THE LONELY LAW

Center Point
Large Print

This Large Print Book carries the Seal of Approval of N.A.V.H.

THE LONELY LAW

MATT STUART

CENTER POINT LARGE PRINT
THORNDIKE, MAINE

This Center Point Large Print edition
is published in the year 2022 by arrangement with
Golden West Inc.

Originally published in the US by Dodd, Mead.

The text of this Large Print edition is unabridged.
In other aspects, this book may vary
from the original edition.
Printed in the United States of America
on permanent paper sourced using
environmentally responsible foresting methods.
Set in 16-point Times New Roman type.

ISBN 978-1-63808-494-5 (hardcover)
ISBN 978-1-63808-498-3 (paperback)

The Library of Congress has cataloged this record
under Library of Congress Control Number: 2022940719

THE LONELY LAW

1

Standing in a pocket of shadow at the corner of the stable of the Soldier Creek stage station, Jim Larribee watched the Medicine Lake stage roll in through the high desert's purple twilight. The team of six was stretched out and running, the gaunt shape of the Concord bucking and swaying behind them. In the doorway of the main station building across the road, Tade Smith showed, had his look, then lifted a short call.

"All right, Howie!"

A hostler gave gruff answer and shuffled over from the stable. The stage pulled to a halt with a trample of dusty hoofs and the dry squeal of brake blocks. The driver tossed the reins down to the hostler, then climbed from the box and headed for the station-house door, lofting a few curt words across his shoulder.

"Last chance for grub this side of McDowell Junction. You got half an hour."

Three passengers, all men, emerged from the stage. One of them tipped a whisky bottle, found it empty, cursed and flung it aside. He squared around on unsteady legs and called thickly after the driver.

"Where do we stop for the night? When do we sleep?"

The driver answered without looking back.

"A lot of dry, hot country between here and McDowell Junction, and it travels easier and cooler after sundown than after sunrise. You can do your sleeping along the way."

The hostler unhitched the team and the horses pushed and crowded on their way to the stable, eager for a roll in the corral dust, for a drink at the creek backwater, and then a manger full of wild timothy. They left behind them a gust of animal heat and the acid odor of their sweat.

Now the roadway lay empty and still, and all the world was in shadow, with the blue dusk smoking up thicker by the minute. Over across the way, lamplight bloomed, thin and yellow in the door and windows of the station. Lured by approaching night, a little wind came down out of the hills and ran off across the flats, striking up small curls of dust.

Stoically patient, Jim Larribee held his place at the stable corner, all his attention now to his right, where the switch-back road that came down off the north point above the canyon mouth curved to cross the creek and angle up past the far side of the stable and corral.

Over there sounded presently a subdued splashing and the faint racket of wheels skidding and jouncing on creek rocks. A buckboard rolled into view, the white points of its team of sorrels showing pale through the gloom. The rig pulled to a halt near the stage and, as it did, Larribee stepped into the clear and moved across the road, sending curtly dry words reaching ahead of him.

"So much for the Gentry word of honor, eh Fitch?"

There was a soft cry by the girl driving the rig. Then came Fitch Gentry's startled words, tight and bitter.

"Larribee! You damned bloodhound! Where'd you come from?"

"More than one way across the hills. I've been waiting for you." Abruptly, Larribee's tone turned rough. "Just how worthless can a Gentry get, anyhow?"

Fitch Gentry made harsh retort.

"Never mind about the Gentrys. Who are you to preach? Mister Jim Larribee, high sheriff of Pinnacle County. But owned from ears to hocks by Big Dan Sharples. When Big Dan snaps the whip, you bark and roll over, just like all the rest of the trained dogs. So, what makes you so damned proud? And now that you're here and I'm here, what do you propose to do about it?"

"Hustle you back to Silver Ford, of course. And this time, bad leg or no bad leg, jail is where you stay!"

There was a moment of silence, of poised physical stillness, there in the thickening dusk. Then came a quick shift of movement by Fitch Gentry, and his hard, explosive defiance.

"Well, now—maybe you do and maybe you don't—!"

The girl's alarm was a protesting echo. "No, Fitch—no!" She caught at his arm.

Jim Larribee had pressed steadily in on the buckboard, and now he covered the final yard or two with a driving lunge that put his grip on Gentry. Swinging his full weight as leverage he hauled Fitch out and down. Falling, Fitch let go a shot from the gun he'd drawn. But the girl had a hand on his arm, dragging at it.

The slug barely missed Larribee, ripping a harmless crater in the road's deep dust, while the report hammered against the front of the station building and bounced off to spread its echo across the deepening night.

Spooked by the shot, the buckboard team hit their collars wildly, taking the rig a good fifty yards along the road before the girl, by sawing at the reins and riding the brake, brought them under control again.

Fitch Gentry landed heavily, face down in the dust, and Larribee dropped on him with bunched and driving knees. He caught at the gun and yanked it from Fitch's weakened grasp. Then he let his anger break gustily.

"This winds it up! I got the proper answer for you!"

He pocketed the gun, dragged Fitch to his feet and pushed him, limping and stumbling, back to where a saddle mount waited, ground-reined beside the stable. From saddlebags Larribee produced handcuffs. Fitch tried to fight him off.

Larribee roughed his man, slamming him against the side of the stable and holding him there with the point of a leaning, hard-braced shoulder. He hauled Fitch's wrists together and snapped the manacles in place. Fitch cursed him with a thin venom.

Larribee shook his prisoner savagely. "Shut up! Close your mouth or I'll fill it with a fist!"

He jerked Fitch away from the stable, spun him around and sent him limping back to the side of the road, across from where men, drawn by that single gunshot, had gathered in front of the stage station. The hostler, bringing up a fresh hitch of six from the stable, had a question thrown at him.

"How about that shot, Howie?"

"A rig comes in off the canyon road," answered Howie. "Right after, there's a shot. But I don't know who and I don't know why."

Larribee sent his call across the dark. "Smith—Tade Smith!"

The answer came, startled. "Yeah! Name yourself."

"Jim Larribee. I'm bringing somebody in I want you to keep an eye on for a few minutes."

"All right."

Some of the defiance drained out of Fitch

Gentry. "You can't take me in there with these damned handcuffs on."

Larribee was adamant. "Just as you are. Get going!"

With dragging step, Fitch Gentry went by the group of curious ones at the station-house door into the light of the room beyond, which combined a short bar and a place to eat. Tade Smith, lumpy, untidy, slack-faced, exclaimed gustily at sight of Larribee's disheveled, sullen prisoner.

"God sakes! Fitch Gentry—in irons! Now what will old Tasker Gentry have to say about this?"

Larribee shrugged impatiently. "Who cares? Let me worry about that."

"The shot?" Smith asked.

"Intended for me," said Larribee. "He tried it—but missed."

He went out and tramped along the road to where the buckboard stood, the team now quiet under the girl's soothing handling. Above the humped-up, blue-black run of the Sabine Hills, early stars showed their first pale shining, and against the silver gleam of these the girl was a subdued, rather forlorn figure, an effect completely lost on Jim Larribee because of the bleak anger boiling in him. He spoke with greater harshness than he realized.

"Girl—where's your common sense? You,

Kelsey Fredericks, mixing in a mess like this! Why did you do it?"

For some little time she did not answer. When she did, her words were low and muffled.

"I had no idea he had a gun. When he drew it, I did my best . . ."

"Sure you did," Larribee admitted gruffly. "You grabbed his arm and made him miss me. My thanks for that. But for being here at all—! You any idea the talk and gossip you've left yourself open to? You, the daughter of John Fredericks, helping such as Fitch Gentry try to pull a runout!"

The lash of his tone and words finally struck fire. Her head lifted and her shoulders squared.

"The daughter of John Fredericks is quite capable of caring for herself and her reputation."

"Not from what I've just seen. You must have known what Fitch intended, breaking the sworn word he gave to Judge Ingalls. Yet you set out to help him do it, and you're not that sort of person at all. Why did you do this?"

"For reasons entirely my own," she flared. "And no concern of yours."

Larribee stared up at her for a moment, then shrugged and gave stern order.

"Turn this rig around and drive back to the stable. The team can stand a graining before we head out across the Sabines again. And we'll need some supper ourselves."

"You needn't concern yourself about either

me or the team," she said stiffly. "As for starting back tonight, I'm not!"

Larribee's sternness deepened. "Oh, yes you are. Right along with Gentry and me. In this buckboard, just as you came."

"You can't make me go. You've no right."

"I have the right and I can make you go. I could arrest you as accessory to Gentry's attempted runout. This is one time when Miss Kelsey Fredericks can't defy everything and everyone and get away with it. Now, are you going to show some sense or do I have to get rough with you too?"

"You wouldn't dare!"

Larribee wiped a weary hand across his face, reaching for patience and not finding any great amount of it.

"You," he said, "will drive this rig back to the stable or I'll do it myself."

She neither answered or moved, her defiance a silent challenge which he accepted with sweeping ruthlessness. He swung up beside her and pulled the reins out of her hands. He slid an arm around her and lifted her to the other end of the seat. He kicked off the brake, hauled the team around and headed back for the stable.

On the seat beside him, Kelsey Fredericks seethed.

"You put rough hands on me!" she gritted furiously. "If I had a gun, I'd—!"

The short-barreled sneak gun he'd taken away from Fitch Gentry was still in Larribee's hip pocket. He pulled it out and dropped it on the seat between them.

"There's a gun. The one Gentry tried to kill me with. If you really feel the same way, go ahead and try your luck. This close, you can't miss."

She did not answer. Neither did she make any move toward touching the weapon.

The hostler was almost done with hooking the fresh team to the stage when Larribee pulled up beside him.

"What's the chance of graining these sorrels and my saddle bronc, Howie?"

Howie answered from the dark. "Where's your horse?"

"Over by the stable."

"You puttin' up here for the night?"

"No. Heading out in a couple of hours."

"Fair enough," Howie said. "I'll take care of things soon as the stage rolls."

Larribee drove on to the stable, tethered the team to a tie ring set in the front wall of the place. He jacked the shells from Fitch Gentry's gun and tucked the empty weapon under the edge of the folded blanket that cushioned the buckboard seat.

"Now," he told Kelsey Fredericks, "we go eat."

"No," she said. "I'm not hungry. I'm staying here."

"Wrong. You're coming with me if I have to carry you."

She climbed down from the buckboard, furious. "How hateful can you be!"

He shrugged. "However you make it necessary."

For a little way she marched beside him, bristling. Then she began to lag and a trace of falter crept into her voice.

"If you make me go in there, I'll be seen and stared at. But if you let—if I stayed out here in the buckboard, they wouldn't know I was here."

"Not that simple," Larribee told her. "They already know you're here. Did you actually think you could haul Fitch Gentry across the Sabines and put him on the stage without anyone knowing how he got here and who brought him? The trouble is, of course, you didn't think in the first place. Now you got to face the music."

She flinched a little as they stepped into the outpour of light from the station door, but when they crossed the threshold, her head was high, her chin defiant.

Fitch Gentry was in a chair in the far corner, hunched forward, his manacled wrists sagging between his knees. The dust of the road was splashed all up and down the front of him and there was a smear of blood about his mouth. His hair had fallen across his forehead and from under it his eyes burned out, hot and sullen. He showed just a flicker of attention when Larribee and the girl came in, then stared straight ahead once more.

Tade Smith's wife, a quarter-blood Shoshone, was serving food to the stage driver and his three passengers, while Smith himself was behind the short bar, pouring drinks for a couple of lank saddle hands from one of the hard scrabble desert outfits. Larribee caught Smith's eye, indicating the girl, Fitch Gentry and himself.

"We'll eat, Tade."

Smith nodded, spoke to his wife and she padded out to the kitchen. Larribee pushed a chair to a table for Kelsey Fredericks, then looked at Gentry.

"You too, Fitch!"

Fitch's head came up and he looked his cold hate. He made no other move.

"A long drag back across the Sabines," Larribee reminded. "Better get smart."

Fitch lifted his hands, fists clenched. The cold metal encircling his wrists gleamed and clinked softly.

"You expect a man to eat with these things on?" he demanded thickly.

"You'll make out if you try."

"I'll starve in hell, first!"

"Just so." Larribee's retort was crisp. "Around midnight tonight you'll be wishing you hadn't been quite so proud."

With high, square shoulders above the long, wiry length of him, Jim Larribee stood as a somewhat gaunt figure. His hard angled face, shadowed with a remote soberness, was deep-stained by wind and sun. His gray eyes were level and penetrating, and carried in their far back depths a glint of wariness, suggesting that here was one who, because of a somewhat cynical skepticism regarding the real motives of others, preferred to stand alone and apart. His boots were scuffed, his jeans worn and his faded shirt was patched at both elbows. But there was no sign of tarnish on the star pinned to his shirt.

Now he eyed Fitch for a moment, speculation in his glance. Then, as he lowered himself into his chair, he nodded, as though confirming some decision he'd made.

"When the time comes, you'll eat."

The stage driver finished with his meal, drained the final drops from his coffee cup with a noisy sipping, then rose and headed for the door where he paused to pack his pipe.

"We're about due to roll," he warned.

His passengers, gulping a final mouthful or two, rose to follow him. The one who had been sucking on the whisky bottle when the stage first pulled in stared boldly at Kelsey Fredericks. He stopped by Larribee's table and leered down at Kelsey's averted head.

"Was I packin' that star, this is the one I'd put

the irons on. This one is really worth hangin' on to!"

As he spoke, he started to drop a hand on Kelsey's shoulder.

All in one deliberate, yet deceptively fast move Jim Larribee knocked the hand aside and came to his feet. His lips had suddenly flattened against his teeth and his eyes had gone arctic with chill. He grabbed the fellow by the shirt front, high up, and squared him around. Then, four flashing times, his right hand ripped across and back. The sound of his hard, callused palm against gross cheeks was a wicked spatting and, under the impacts, welts, broad and crimson, leaped into being. He ended by half throwing, half shoving the fellow toward the door, following him with savage words.

"Get out!"

Stumbling, his mouth leaking crimson, the man floundered through the door. The stage driver, never missing a puff as he cuddled a flaring match in the curve of one hand and passed it back and forth across the bowl of his pipe, peered through the smoke at Larribee with squinting, approving eyes. He waved the match stub up and down to put it out, then made dry comment.

"I've seen it happen before. The fools with the big mouths never seem to learn. All right—I said we roll!"

He moved on into the dark and the two

remaining passengers hurried after him. A few moments later a whip cracked, a thinly urging, high-pitched "Ya-a-a-h!" echoed, and then came the riffle of running hoofs, the dust-muffled clack of wheels, and the stage was gone into night's deep distance.

Taking his chair again, Jim Larribee was met with Kelsey Fredericks' low-voiced, furious words.

"Was that necessary?"

"I thought so." The curtness of aroused feeling was in Larribee's reply. "That whelp would have put his dirty hands on you."

Her handsome head was up now, her eyes bright with the anger of her embarrassment. Slightly high cheekbones gave a tapered effect to her face. It was an alert face, smoothly brown. Under the lamplight her hair was dark and fine and glossy.

"A few minutes ago you expressed all kinds of concern over the reputation of John Fredericks' daughter. Do you think you did it any good by striking up that brawl?"

He shrugged a little wearily. "No brawl, though call it what you like. All I know is the wrong person said the wrong thing and made the wrong move toward you. I got no better answer than that."

She flashed a quick glance at him, eying him with a grave intentness, which was lost on Larribee, because now he was looking at Fitch Gentry, and the churned-up feeling in him roughened his tone.

"I said you were going to eat, Gentry. You better get up here. Don't make me come after you!"

Fitch got into sullen movement, limped over to the table and slid sideways into a chair. Tade Smith's wife brought their food. It was coarse fare, but it was hot and savory and good, and Jim Larribee, whipped by a hunger sixteen-hours old, went at his with frank eagerness. The lure of steaming coffee and fragrance of warm food stirred up the real hunger in Kelsey Fredericks and Fitch Gentry, too, and they were soon doing their share, Fitch managing very well despite the handcuffs, once he put his mind to it.

Replete, Larribee leaned back, thumbed tobacco and papers from the pocket of his shirt, built a cigarette. Noting Fitch eying the smoke hungrily, he built another and handed it across, then scratched a match for both.

"Now," he said, "we got nothing to do but take it easy for an hour or so."

The desert riders had carried their glasses and a deck of dog-eared cards over to one of the tables and began a game of pedro, betting quarters. They played in a grave quiet, speaking seldom, and then only in low toned monosyllables.

Knowing the high desert, Jim Larribee knew

how it was with men like these. Line riders, most likely, who had come far just to spend an evening here at Soldier Creek. Drab as this place was, it still offered something different than an isolated, lonely line camp.

Here they could burn their throats with a few shots of Tade Smith's whisky, eat a meal cooked by someone beside themselves, be on hand when the stage rolled through and so, perhaps, glean a morsel or two of news to carry away with them to ponder and discuss until they had worn it down to the last threadbare bone. Yet, Larribee knew, it was just such frugal intervals of change as this that kept lonely men from going completely sour.

Well, he reflected wryly, they'd have enough talking material now to last them a very considerable time. Through them, the desert would get word of the law putting handcuffs on Fitch Gentry, old Tasker Gentry's son. And also that the handsome daughter of John Fredericks was mixed up in the picture somewhere. It wouldn't be spread in the light of malicious gossip, but it was news in a news-hungry land, and so it would be spread. And there was no help for it.

Howie, fusty and untidy from the stable, came in. He looked at Larribee.

"The sorrels and that buckskin of yours got the nosebags on. I figger they'll be eatin' right on two dollars' worth of oats. Do I collect from you or the county?"

“Strikes me that’s quite a lot of oats, Howie,” Larribee said drily.

Howie’s grin was small and sly. “What’s the county for if it ain’t to be gouged? Ain’t really comin’ out of your pocket; you’ll get it back. And a man’s entitled to a little somethin’ extra for his work.”

“Sure, Howie—sure.” Larribee dug two silver dollars from a pocket and flipped them, one after the other, spinning through the air. Howie caught both coins deftly.

Larribee turned to Kelsey Fredericks and said almost gently, “There’s time for you to catch a few winks before we pull out.”

“You needn’t concern yourself.”

He shrugged, left the table and took a chair over against the far wall, slouching down, letting his whole rawboned length sag in complete relaxation. He tipped his hat low over his eyes against the reach of the lamplight and then went utterly still.

Kelsey Fredericks and Fitch Gentry kept their seats at the table. Tade Smith’s wife came in and cleared away the dishes, her black eyes touching Kelsey several times with quick, flitting glances of feminine curiosity. Twice Fitch muttered some remark to Kelsey. Each time she made no verbal reply, just shook her head in sharp negation. Fitch slid down in his chair and lost himself in surly, glowering silence.

Time slipped by. Night's chill, pressing down from the hills, moved in through the open door, and Tade Smith went over and swung the portal shut. He glanced at Jim Larribee's motionless figure, seemed about to speak, then shrugged and turned away, going over to watch the line riders at their pedro game.

Observing narrowly from shadowed eyes, Larribee saw the combative stiffness seep out of Kelsey Fredericks' back and shoulders, saw her droop a little, and knew there was weariness in her she could not deny. The balance of this night was going to be rough on her. The miles would seem endlessly long, the hours even more so. And there would be no comfort at all in riding them both out.

For a little time he played with the thought of spending the night here at Soldier Creek, giving her a chance to rest. But in the end he pushed this softening thought aside, reflecting grimly that every time he'd shown generosity to either a Gentry or a Fredericks, he'd been taken advantage of.

The line riders finished a final pedro game. Yawning, Tade Smith poured one on the house to make the dark trail home seem a little shorter. They drank, then went out into the night, flashing the hungry yet respectful glances of lonely men at Kelsey Fredericks as they passed.

Jim Larribee went over to the bar, slid some

money across, made low-toned comment to Tade Smith, who nodded and went out back somewhere. Larribee turned to the pair at the table.

"Time to go."

Fitch Gentry got sullenly to his feet. Kelsey Fredericks looked up at Larribee. Weariness had drawn at the curve of her lips and had put something not far from wistfulness in her eyes. Sight of these things dragged at Larribee's decision to leave. Then he again pushed this momentary compassion aside, and the old wariness rose in him.

Quick as this reaction had been, it was not fast enough to keep Kelsey from seeing and recognizing both the flicker of sympathy and the wariness that wiped it out. A faint flush stained her cheek, and when she stood up, all the first defiance and pride again showed in the erectness of her shoulders and the cast of her head. Larribee moved to take her arm as they stepped out into the night, but she pulled quickly away and marched along by herself under the cold stars.

Over at the buckboard, Tade Smith was stowing a bundle in the back of the rig. He murmured acceptance of Larribee's thanks, then drifted away. Larribee's voice sharpened as he spoke to Fitch Gentry.

"Over here!"

He put Fitch up on the near end of the buckboard seat, unlocked the handcuff steel from Fitch's right wrist, then pulled his left arm down and snapped the empty half of the manacle around the iron seat brace.

"Like a dog on a chain," complained Fitch bitterly.

"Just so," agreed Larribee. "And remember, you brought it on yourself."

He put his buckskin saddle bronc at lead behind the rig. Rolled up in back of his saddle cantle was his fleece-lined coat. He loosed the tie strings, shook the garment out and turned to Kelsey Fredericks.

"Better crawl into this. Some long, cold hours ahead."

She was dressed in a light woolen blouse and a divided skirt of twill, little enough to face the chill of night in. Yet she answered as she had before.

"Don't concern yourself."

"Fair enough," shrugged Larribee, donning the coat himself. "You'll probably change your mind, later."

With the girl sitting between Fitch Gentry and himself, he brought the sorrels away from the front of the stable in a short sweep, then turned into the canyon road.

Ahead lifted the Sabine Hills, black and cold.

2

With his long, thin legs at full stretch in front of him, and the burly bulk of his body cramming the round-backed chair to capacity, Big Dan Sharples sat on the porch of his sprawling Acme Mercantile establishment and watched the softening haze of twilight wrap around the town of Silver Ford. Behind thick lids which drooped at their outer corners, his small, cold eyes were speculative with thought, and presently, rolling his after-supper cigar across heavy lips, he cleared his throat and spoke in husky tones.

"Curly, I want to see Ed Forbush tonight. Dobe, you locate Carter and Redstone and bring them around."

They had been squatting on their heels against the wall beside Big Dan's chair: Dobe Lear and Curly Gibson; Dobe, thin and waspy, with a brown paper cigarette ever sagging at one corner of his tight-lipped mouth. Curly Gibson was a bigger man, with a stolid, never-changing brutality squaring his face.

Lifting to their feet now, they drifted wordlessly away, Dobe taking a final drag at his cigarette then flipping it aside, the butt tracing a curving line of crimson against the dusk before dying in the dust of the street in a tiny swirl of sparks.

This town of Silver Ford roughly centered the long running miles of the valley of the Pride River. Built on the west side of the river, it was a town of two streets, both lined with the tall, tapered grace of lombardy poplar trees. The east end of River Street dipped in at the shallow river crossing that gave the town its name. Valley Street ran north and south. The core of the town was grouped around the four corners formed by the junction of the streets.

The Acme Mercantile stood north of River Street and west of Valley, while cater-cornered across the street junction the two-storied bulk of the Riverview Hotel lifted. Now, out of the Riverview, Grant Hilliker stepped, pausing to light a cigar before making his walk over to the store in his brisk, quick striding way. A lawyer, he was a slim, taut man, with cool eyes and a rapier mind. He climbed the low steps and moved even with Sharples.

Watching the lawyer approach, Big Dan had drawn back his extended legs and straightened in his chair. But his heavy shoulders were hunched in an attitude of unconscious hostility, with his head pulled down between them. His husky toned words brought Hilliker to a halt.

"A minute, Grant. Been wanting a talk with you."

"Yes?" said Hilliker.

"About Jim Larribee."

"What about him?"

"Why," said Big Dan, "it comes to me that you've been trying to give him some advice. The wrong kind."

The tip of Hilliker's cigar glowed ruby red as he drew strongly on it.

"Meaning—?"

"You know damned well what I mean!" Big Dan's tone roughened. "I suggest you quit trying to put ideas into Larribee's head. He's my man. I made him and he works for me. You start remembering that!"

Grant Hilliker looked down at Sharples, silent for a long moment while he rocked back and forth from heel to toe and puffed at his cigar. When he finally spoke, his words were soft.

"I wonder if you realize how that sounds? Carrying the star, Jim Larribee represents the law in this county. When you call him your man you are, in effect, saying that you own that law. Such talk is not only damned nonsense, but stupidly arrogant as well. Also and mainly, so far as I'm concerned, grossly unfair to Jim. As his friend, I resent it."

"Resent and be damned!" Big Dan leaned combatively forward. "I'm the only real friend Jim Larribee ever had around here. When John Fredericks and Tasker Gentry busted him and run him off Concho Creek, who was it picked him up, loaned him money to tide him over, put some fight back in him and made a sheriff out of him? I did! Me—Dan Sharples! So you bet he's my man. And you lay off him with your high and fancy talk."

Hilliker took the cigar from his lips, stared at the half inch of ash that had formed on the tip of it. Again when he spoke his words were soft, holding now a faint thread of wonderment.

"You amaze me, you really do. You, Dan Sharples, would be God! Oh, I admit you've done right well by Dan Sharples, though by methods impossibly crude. You've made virtual dogs of several men. You'd do the same with Jim Larribee. That, of course, I will do all in my power to prevent!"

"You've been warned." Blunt, thick-throated threat was in Big Dan's words. "Leave Larribee alone!"

"No," Hilliker said evenly. "No, I won't leave him alone. You claim Jim Larribee as your man. I claim him as my friend. There's a wide distinction between the two. In your own manner of speaking, Dan—to hell with you!"

So saying, Grant Hilliker knocked the ash from his cigar, letting it spill down onto Big Dan's lap. It was a move of utter contempt. Then the lawyer moved on into the store, where old Charley Clark was fussing at the mail rack under a down-pouring cone of yellow lamplight. Wordlessly, the old fellow handed a small bundle of mail to

Hilliker, who pocketed it, thanked him with a nod, then left as briskly as he had entered.

Big Dan was on his feet now, standing with a shoulder point against one of the porch posts. With his long, bony legs and thick upper body, he made a strangely top-heavy figure. He watched in silence as Grant Hilliker moved through evening's ever deepening gloom to Tom Ivy's Maverick Bar, directly across Valley Street, showing briefly there in sharp silhouette as he pushed through the swinging doors.

Big Dan, sucking at his cigar butt, found it dead, tossed it away and turned back into the store, there to speak a brief word to Charley Clark.

"All for tonight, Charley. Close up!"

He went through a rear door to his bachelor quarters out back. Here a lamp, turned low, burned on the living-room table. He lengthened the wick of the lamp, then began pacing back and forth in the reaching light, his shadow huge and misshapen against the walls.

There was much about this man that bordered on the grotesque. The strange build of him, with those long, thin legs supporting a thick, almost ponderous body. In his stride there was the suggestion of a high-kneed shuffle, while his arms dangled and swung loosely. His face was broad, with a freckled skin pulled dry and tight across heavy cheekbones. His nose was coarse, with thick, flaring nostrils, and under it his lips were stacked, one upon the other, in two fleshy rolls. His roan hair, close cropped, stood up in a coarse, stiff roach. This man was ugly, and he was misshapen, but he was a power in this town of Silver Ford, and all up and down the county.

Charley Clark, done with locking up, came in with the cash box, which he put on the table, then stood waiting for any further orders. Big Dan shook his head, so Charley let himself out of the rear kitchen door into the night. Now all the big, sprawling building, combining store, warehouse and living quarters, fell quiet, except for the occasional creak of a floor board under Big Dan's measured pacing.

His thoughts on Grant Hilliker, Big Dan went over what the lawyer had said and how he had said it, and the way he had flicked his cigar ash, and the memory built up a black and grinding edge of anger that kept him restless and prowling.

Finally quieting, he took the cash box over to the old-fashioned, riveted iron safe that stood in a corner of the room. He put the cash box inside, started to close the safe, hesitated, and then from a small drawer took out the tintype picture of a young woman's laughing face; a pretty, spirited face, framed in a luxury of loose-tossed hair.

For some little time Big Dan studied the picture, heavily brooding. Then he restored the picture to the drawer, closed and locked the safe door, then took the lamp off the table and went into the kitchen.

Here a coffeepot murmured gently on the stove. Big Dan poured himself a cup, slugged it generously with whisky, lighted a fresh cigar, pulled up a chair and settled back to wait. The coffee royal was gone, a second nearly so, before a knock sounded at the rear kitchen door and Big Dan's growling summons let in Dobe Lear and two others.

Along with Big Dan himself, these two, Bert Carter and Ira Redstone, made up the board of county commissioners. Ira Redstone owned the stage and freighting business that connected Silver Ford with Medicine Lake, and so to the outside world. Bert Carter ran the Riverside Hotel and posed as its owner. Only Carter and Big Dan knew whose money was really behind the hotel, and it wasn't Carter's.

Redstone and Carter were typical small-caliber politicians. Where they thought it safe they could be arrogant. But they were equally quick to bend the knee when and where it counted. For several years they had been bending it to Big Dan Sharples, for his favor was their political and financial lives, which they well understood. So Bert Carter and Ira Redstone cut the cloth of their official business exactly to the pattern of Big Dan's wishes.

Now they pulled up chairs, while Dobe Lear

waited a little time. When Big Dan gave him no further instructions, he said:

"I'll be over at the Maverick."

Big Dan nodded and Dobe slipped out. Big Dan knew exactly what the waspy man would do. He'd sit in a corner of Tom Ivy's Maverick Bar and nurse a couple of drinks all evening. Tomorrow, if asked, he'd give an accurate account of all that went on in the place. Who drank there and who didn't. What things were discussed and by whom. He'd know men's opinions and their ideas. Along with other shadings of value, Dobe Lear was a faithful and reliable extra pair of eyes and ears to Big Dan.

Big Dan let Carter and Redstone hang in speculation for some time before making abrupt announcement.

"I'm moving Ed Forbush up on to Concho Creek tomorrow."

Both men flinched and Bert Carter exclaimed: "Dan, that will break the old trouble wide open again. There'll be hell to pay!"

To this Ira Redstone gave quick support.

"It would be a mistake to bring that old argument back to life again."

Big Dan drained the contents of his cup, wiped his lips with the back of his hand and ran a freshening match across the end of his cigar. Then he spoke bluntly.

"Not a question of bringing anything back to

life. The Concho Creek argument has never been dead."

Carter persisted. "John Fredericks and Tasker Gentry beat you at Concho Creek before, Dan."

Darkness shaded Big Dan's face and his voice was an eruptive growl.

"They didn't beat me. Nobody ever beats me. All Fredericks and Gentry did was to stall off, for a little time, my beating them. They had their own man, Boardy Samuels, in as sheriff. That was what made the difference, then. Now I got my man in. Jim Larribee. Now I'll call the turns."

Ira Redstone shifted restlessly. He was a florid, thick-set man, stolidly unimaginative, whose active thinking was pretty much grooved to the limits of his stage and freighting business. But on occasion he could show stubbornness.

"What worth is there in stirring up trouble? Say you do put Forbush on Concho Creek and make it stick this time, what does it gain you?"

"Maybe a lot of things you'd never understand," Big Dan said curtly.

"Well, I don't like it," Redstone blurted. "I just don't like it."

Big Dan stared at him with a fixity that presently beat down Redstone's eyes, made him shift his glance. Color filled his cheeks, as both shame and anger ran through him; anger at Big Dan for cowing him, anger and shame at himself for being cowed.

Big Dan swung his glance at Bert Carter. "Maybe you're going to try and tell me my business too?"

Carter, lean and hatchet-faced, gave hurried assurance.

"Not at all, Dan—not at all. Only, things have been running so smooth, I thought—"

"You let me do the thinking," cut in Big Dan bruskly. "If I want suggestions, I'll ask for them. I didn't call you in here tonight to start offering any."

"Mind saying just why you did want us?" Redstone asked, sulky and silently resisting.

Big Dan rolled his cigar in his fingers and lips and drew deeply on it, while his eyes lay heavy lidded and cold on Ira Redstone's face.

"You know, Ira, there's one hell of a lot of stuff moves through this place of mine in the course of a year. I was checking up the other day and found I'd paid you right on three thousand dollars last year in hauling and freighting fees. Now that's a fair chunk of money, and it set me to thinking that it might pay me to put on a couple of freight outfits of my own, and do my own hauling.

"By picking up a little extra outside freight along the way, I could show a profit all around. The more I play with the idea, the more it appeals to me. Be real interesting, don't you think, you and me competing for the freight business all along the Pride River Valley? Nothing like competition, they say, to make things interesting."

Listening, much of the heavy color faded from Ira Redstone's face. He essayed a laugh, but it carried little mirth.

"You do like your little joke, eh Dan?"

"Joke be damned! You won't think it's a joke if I go through with it. So you want to know why I brought you here. All right, here it is. When Gentry and Fredericks find Ed Forbush sitting on Concho Creek, they're going to get ideas of playing it rough. When they do, they'll find Jim Larribee looking right down their throats. Outside of killing him, which they'll hesitate at, there is only one way they can do Larribee harm. That would be by getting him in bad with the county commissioners. Us!"

Big Dan paused, chewing at his cigar before going on.

"They certainly won't come to me. But they may have a try at you two. If they do, I expect you to stand fast. I don't care if they come at you with entreaty, prayer, money or threat. You stand fast! Remember, Jim Larribee is my man. I put him where he is and I want him kept there. Understand?"

They nodded; Ira Redstone silently, Bert Carter following with nervous words.

"Sure, Dan—sure! Jim Larribee's doing a fine job as sheriff."

"That," said Big Dan, banging a fist on the table for emphasis, "is the exact and only answer I want you two to give out to anybody who comes crying to you. So, we understand each other there. Now here is one more thing. Ira, this is for you. One week from tonight I want two of your freight outfits at Trent's Meadow."

Redstone's head swung up, startled. "Trent's Meadow! What in hell is there to haul at Trent's Meadow?"

"That you'll find out at the time. Just—have those rigs there. And don't talk about it to anybody. Got it?"

Redstone nodded. "Trent's Meadow. That's out along the old White Pine Road, isn't it?"

"Right! And pretty well back from the main valley. Remember, no talk. Not even to your skinners. Don't let them know where they're going until they get there. You lead the way in a buckboard. I'll give you all the details later. Handle the job right and I'll forget all about going into the freighting business. Now, how about a little drink?"

Fortified by the feed of oats and a couple of hours' rest, the sorrels took the buckboard away from Soldier Creek with a rush. They were running when they hit the creek crossing and the spray flew high. Some of it struck the faces of the buckboard's occupants and, beside him, Jim

Larribee heard Kelsey Fredericks gasp and felt her recoil from the icy, hard-driven touch.

By the time they had worked out the switchbacks of the canyon road and reached the higher run of it, the sorrels had spent their first exuberance and were settled to an even pace, and from time to time a gust of their animal warmth came back to those on the buckboard seat.

This was, however, but a mocking reminder of the night's brittle mood. Coming out of the canyon they had climbed through air laden with the creek's damp, after dark chill. Now, though they had moved away from that, they were up where the night wind, fresh down from some far loftiness, met them head on, and Kelsey Fredericks began waging a losing fight against its increasingly frigid breath.

By clenching her teeth she managed to keep them from chattering, but there was no way she could avoid the sudden, violent shiver that ran abruptly through her. Nor could she, riding shoulder to shoulder with Jim Larribee, hide this from him. In consequence, he rode the brake and pulled the sorrels to a halt. He shrugged out of his coat.

"Put this on," he ordered bruskly. "And no argument."

There was none. Pure physical misery overrode defiant pride. The garment was full of the warmth of his occupancy, and she snuggled down into it gratefully. From its depths her voice came up in a faintly apologetic murmur.

"Now you'll suffer. I—I feel guilty."

It was on Jim Larribee's tongue to tell her it was high time she felt something of the sort, but he held back all words except a gruff:

"Forget it!"

For some distance the road followed along the canyon rim, then cut away across the high, rolling benchland country toward a distant gap that marked the final backbone of the hills. It crossed open parks and meadows and tunneled for long stretches through heavy timber, where the resinous breath of the forest was layered so thickly it left a flavor on a man's tongue.

But for the mutter of hoofs, the occasional jangle of a trace or the low squeal of an iron-shod buckboard wheel across a rock surface of some kind, it was a silent ride. Weariness began working its way with both horses and humans.

Wedged in between Jim Larribee on her right and Fitch Gentry on her left, Kelsey Fredericks sagged deeper and deeper into the folds of Larribee's coat, and, lured by its warmth, began to nod. Twice she straightened with a jerk, shaking her head, trying to fight off the drowsiness. In the end it was too much for her, and presently her cheek settled against Larribee's shoulder and she slept.

During the slow, cold hours of early morning,

a misshapen moon crept up in the east and in the furtive light of this the buckboard rolled through that once distant gap in the hill summit and began dropping down the timbered slope beyond into the high valley of the Pride River. Dawn's first grayness was sifting across the world when the road broke from the timber into a small clearing where a stand of aspens marked the presence of a water seep. Here, too, was a blackened area against the earth where fires had been built before.

Jim Larribee pulled over to the aspens and stopped. Cessation of the buckboard's motion awakened Kelsey Fredericks. For a moment or two she did not move, her cheek warm against Larribee's shoulder. Then she jerked erect and stammered her confusion.

"I—I did not mean—I had no idea—!"

"It's quite all right," Larribee said dryly. "We rest here and coffee up."

He climbed down from the rig, turned and held up an aiding hand. Either because she was half asleep and too confused to see it, or because she chose deliberately to ignore it, she did not accept the offer of the steadying hand. In consequence, stiff and uncertain from cold and cramped inactivity, her reaching foot missed the buckboard step and she'd have gone flat on her face but for the quick, containing sweep of Jim Larribee's arm. For a moment she lay against him, startled, breathless—jarred thoroughly wide awake. He straightened her up, put her aside, and made blunt comment.

"Still dead set on bumping your stubborn head, aren't you?"

He tramped away along the edge of the timber, kicked aside a pile of forest litter about one end of a down log and came up with a handful of dry duff from a last year's deserted chipmunk's nest. He stacked dry branches expertly about this, struck a match and shortly ruddy flames were beginning to lift and snap cheerily, and the incense of fat pine woodsmoke drifted across the early morning air. Larribee went around the buckboard and unlocked the handcuff from the seat brace.

"All right, Fitch!"

Fitch Gentry had not spoken a word since they left Soldier Creek, and now that same silent sullenness held him. He made no protest as Larribee manacled his free wrist again. He limped over to the fire and hunkered down by its reaching warmth.

Kelsey Fredericks stood across the fire from Fitch. Swathed in Larribee's coat, half lost in its overgenerous folds, she looked like a sleepy, tousled subdued child. On his part, Fitch Gentry's face showed lined and haggard in the firelight.

From the back of the buckboard Larribee brought the sack which Tade Smith had put there at Soldier Creek. It held a coffeepot, some cups, a small bag of coffee. Larribee filled the pot at the seep, poured in coffee, tucked the pot against the fire. Then he settled back on his heels, built a cigarette and stared into the flames. Covertly, Kelsey Fredericks looked down at him.

His face was taciturn and unrevealing, carved in lean bronze by the fireglow. His eyes were deep-shadowed and his lips a level line above the jut of his chin. If night's chill had in any way affected him, he did not show it. His shirt, sagging to the weight of the star pinned to it, was open at the throat, revealing the hard, corded muscles that ran down from the relaxed slope of his shoulders and across his upper chest. Just the faintest hint of fatigue pinched at the corners of his eyes and lips.

At the moment, Kelsey Fredericks decided, he seemed to have forgotten her presence and that of Fitch Gentry completely; he was entirely apart, lost in some far, solitary speculation.

Presently the coffeepot began to bubble and steam and a quickening fragrance lifted. Larribee pulled the pot away from the heat and let the contents settle. He poured a cup for Kelsey and one for Fitch Gentry. He filled one for himself, cradled it in his hands and drank with a keen relish.

It was black and strong and infinitely good at this moment. It was rich and scalding and it warmed them and restored them. Before they were done they had emptied the pot. Larribee doused the fire, rinsed and sacked the utensils, then jerked his head toward the buckboard.

"Once more," he said. "Next stop—Silver Ford."

Fitch Gentry pushed stiffly to his feet, turned toward the rig, then stopped short, head tipped as he listened. Jim Larribee listened, too, drawn up tall and alert. Where nothing had been before, there now was a faint echo, growing stronger. While they listened the echo became a trampling of hoofs. Then, swinging out of the timber and into the road along the edge of the clearing, came a group of riders. Both Fitch Gentry and Kelsey Fredericks exclaimed, but it was Fitch who called hoarsely.

"Boardy—Boardy Samuels! Over here, Boardy!"

The riders came away from the road with a rush, spurring across the opening. Fitch Gentry moved as if to meet them, but Larribee caught him by the arm and swung him back.

"It's not quite that simple, Fitch. Stay put!"

Then Larribee stepped out ahead to face the approaching group and lift a warning hand.

"Close enough until we understand each other!"

One of the group was John Fredericks. Another was Boardy Samuels, once sheriff of Pinnacle County, but now old Tasker Gentry's foreman. The balance were mixed Fredericks and Gentry riders. When they came to a stop, it was John Fredericks who pushed to the front.

He was a square-hewn man, with fine, bold features and a crisp black mustache above a stern mouth. About him lay an air of power and authority that made him appear bigger than he actually was. Unmistakably, there was about him now a still, cold anger, tempered somewhat with relief.

His bleak glance roved from Jim Larribee to Fitch Gentry, then moved to his daughter, Kelsey, where it held for a long moment. After which it came back to Larribee, and the cattleman's voice rang harshly.

"All right, Larribee—you tell it!"

Jim Larribee shrugged.

"When Judge Ingalls let Gentry here out on bail, pending trial for his part in that Ten Mile shooting scrape, he did so on Gentry's plea that his wounded leg wasn't getting proper care in jail. On his sworn promise that he wouldn't get outside the limit of the Gentry ranch without court permission, the judge granted Fitch's plea. Along with Judge Ingalls, I thought even a Gentry would respect his sworn word. We were both wrong. I caught up with this one at Soldier Creek before he could grab the stage for McDowell Junction and parts unknown. That's it!"

John Fredericks nodded curtly, then looked accusingly at his daughter.

"I thought you were visiting Rose Alten. Then it was Rose herself, riding in at the ranch, saying she had come to spend a couple of days with you. I didn't know what to think. I set the crew to scouting and we finally picked up word just a little bit ago that you'd been seen heading this way with Gentry in the rig. We took a look and picked up the wheel tracks—and well—we find you here. In God's name, girl—what was your idea in hauling Fitch out to Soldier Creek? Why did you do it? Why?"

The answer came low and muffled.

"As I think about it now, I—I can't imagine why. At the time it seemed a reasonable thing to do. I thought—perhaps . . ."

"You thought—what?"

She did not answer, but met the impact of her father's anger and accusing eyes with her shoulders straight and her head high.

Watching, Jim Larribee thought: he's giving her silent hell, and she's all raw under the whip of it. But she's not trying to dodge. She's got courage. But her chin is trembling . . .

John Fredericks was insistent. "You thought—what?" he demanded again.

Larribee swung his shoulders in a quick restlessness and spoke bluntly.

"This is hardly the time or place for that sort of thing, Fredericks. After all, a purely generous impulse may not always make sense, but it doesn't hurt to remember that it was—generous."

The words stirred a little catch of breath by Kelsey that was not far from a sob. Also, they brought the grim impact of the cattleman's glance back to Larribee, where it held steadily. When he spoke, there was a hint of gruff apology in Fredericks' tone.

"Maybe you're right."

There was nothing apologetic, however, in either the look or the words John Fredericks now put on Fitch Gentry. Instead, they dripped a cold and cutting contempt.

"All along you made a lot of talk about self-defense in that Ten Mile shoot-out you mixed in, claiming that Price Tedrow went for his gun first. The looks of this makes you out a liar."

Fitch swung his head sullenly and gave out with a mumbled excuse.

"What chance could I figure on against a jury handpicked by Big Dan Sharples and his crowd? Answer me that fair, and you'll know why I pulled out."

"If there was any truth to your self-defense claim, you had nothing to worry about," growled Fredericks bitingly. "And if a man's sworn word means nothing to him, then he's in damn poor shape."

"I tell you I couldn't figure on a square shake," argued Fitch. "You know that . . ."

But John Fredericks wasn't listening. He was speaking to Jim Larribee again.

"How far will you need the buckboard and team?"

"To Silver Ford."

"Fair enough." Fredericks turned to one of his men. "Len, you let Kelsey have your horse. You go along with Larribee and bring the rig home when he's done with it."

Kelsey Fredericks climbed into the saddle from which Len Hobart stepped. She gathered up the reins, then turned her head and looked directly at Jim Larribee. Very softly she spoke two words.

"Thank you!"

She lifted the horse to a run over to the road and along it into the timber. John Fredericks and his riders followed at a lesser pace. Left now, aside from Len Hobart, was only Boardy Samuels and two others of Tasker Gentry's crew.

Looking after John Fredericks, Fitch Gentry began to curse.

"He don't give a thin damn what happens to me. He's supposed to be a good friend of the Gentrys, to play everything close to us. But from the looks of this he's just another damn fair-weather—!"

Jim Larribee broke in impatiently. "Cut it fine, Fitch. Cut it fine! I'm tired of hearing you feel sorry for yourself."

Boardy Samuels, silent spectator to it all until

now, touched his horse with the spur and moved closer.

"You got no right to keep a man from speaking his mind, Larribee. Even with that star on, you ain't God!"

He was a swarthy one, was Boardy Samuels, so dark as to suggest mixed blood of some sort. Once he had worn the star now pinned to Jim Larribee's shirt, and his hate for the man who had succeeded him in office was a thin glitter in his murky eyes.

"No," he said again, "you ain't God!"

Larribee came around to face him. "I told you to keep your distance, Samuels. Back up!"

Instead of complying, Boardy grinned evilly as he looked past Jim Larribee at Fitch Gentry. He gave a meaningful nod and spoke terse, purring words.

"Go ahead, Fitch—go ahead. Hit him!"

3

In facing Boardy Samuels to warn him off, Jim Larribee had put his back to Fitch Gentry. Fitch had no gun. His wrists were manacled. It was reasonable to discount any threat of resistance by him. Yet, at this moment, with Boardy Samuels leering mockingly, Larribee knew the dismal conviction that he'd been outmaneuvered, that he'd made one of the bad mistakes of his life.

He tried desperately to correct it. He tried to side-step and whirl and drag his gun. He was only part way around when Fitch, lips twisted in a grimace of wicked effort, lunged in and brought his high-flung, steel-encircled wrists smashing down.

The impact, even though partly cushioned by the bulk and substance of his hat, filled Jim Larribee's head with stunning shock. Numbness ran through him, drugging all his muscles. The weight of the gun he'd drawn became enormous, far too much for him to hold, and the weapon slid free of his nerveless grasp.

Fitch Gentry kept coming, swinging his arms up and down in another clubbing effort. This blow missed Larribee's head, striking him on the shoulder. After which Fitch drove against him, pushing and mauling, clawing with both hands, while yelling at Boardy Samuels.

"Get at him, Boardy! Goddamn it—get at him!"

Boardy spun his horse in a half turn, left his saddle in a swooping dive. He landed on Larribee's shoulders, and this impact, added to the effect of Fitch's first blow, put Jim Larribee to his knees, where he stayed for a little time while Boardy and Fitch swarmed over him.

Out of some depth of desperation he found strength enough to finally shake clear and gain his feet again. He swung a fist that seemed ponderously slow and futile, yet it landed full on Fitch's mouth, driving him back and bringing a gout of crimson fanning down across his chin.

It was a final and useless effort, for now Boardy Samuels set himself and drove two savage blows to the side of Larribee's head, one landing behind the ear, the other full on the temple. They started Larribee down again and Boardy dug a knee into him as he fell. Half kneeling, half lying on his man, Boardy clubbed Larribee's unprotected jaw again and again. Fitch, crowding in came down once more with the handcuffs. Jim Larribee slid away into blackness.

Fitch pawed at him furiously, panting.

"The key—the key! He's got the key in his pocket—!"

Boardy Samuels found it and a moment later Fitch was able to fling the hated manacles aside. He got to his feet, his mashed lips puffed and bloody.

"Now, by God!" he bawled in malignant triumph. "Now we'll see!"

He drew back his foot, aimed a kick at Jim Larribee's head. Before he could deliver it, Len Hobart's voice rang coldly.

"Hold it! Nothing like that, Gentry. Back away and leave him alone. Both of you!"

Fitch came around, vicious and wild.

"None of your mix, Hobart. Keep out of it!"

"Right!" echoed Boardy Samuels. "Entirely none of your mix."

The grizzle of middle age lay at the temples of Len Hobart. He was a man who had sat saddle leather up and down a lot of trails, some of them pretty rough ones, and they had left their indelible imprint on him. He was a taciturn man, seldom speaking. When he did, he meant what he said.

"You got what you were after. The handcuffs are off. That's enough. Leave him alone!"

"No!" stormed Fitch. "Be damned if I will! I owe him plenty. I got him where I want him and I'm going to work him over—good!"

Len Hobart drew a gun with smooth, effortless, flickering speed.

"You weren't listening close enough, Gentry. Arresting you and bringing you in was Larribee's business, strictly. If he couldn't make it stick, that was his hard luck. But the man is down and out now, and can't protect himself. So, not you or anybody else is going to kick or stomp him around. That's it!"

Boardy Samuels studied Len Hobart with a long, muddy, calculating glance. What he saw convinced him. He shrugged.

"If that's the way you want it, Hobart, I guess that's the way it is." He moved over to his horse and mounted.

Lacking Boardy's support, Fitch began backing away too.

"I ain't walking," he declared sullenly. "I got to ride this bum leg of mine somehow. I'm taking that buckskin bronc of Larribee's."

Len Hobart shook his head. "You can double up with Samuels."

Fitch began to curse again, but Boardy Samuels cut him short with a hard wave of his hand.

"Save it—save it! There's nothing here for us. Come on up!"

So speaking, Boardy kicked his left foot clear, and Fitch, limping over, stepped into the empty stirrup and swung up behind. Boardy Samuels held back for a final word.

"Other days coming, Hobart. Lots of them. Don't get too proud over this one."

He reined away and the other two riders, who had watched and listened to it all in unmoving silence, dropped in beside him. Boardy Samuels said nothing to them, but Fitch poured on the rawhide in harsh, complaining anger. His only answer was a sullen shrugging.

Len Hobart watched them out of sight, then put away his gun and built a cigarette. Through the pale smoke of this he saw Jim Larribee finally begin to stir. But after a first small sign of movement it was several long minutes before Larribee, groaning softly, rolled over and pushed up to his elbows. This way, too, he stayed for some little time, shaking his head to clear it. A line of crimson seeped from his nose and bracketed a corner of his mouth. Hobart could see another stain of crimson trickling in slow drops out of Larribee's hair, from just behind his left ear.

Finally Larribee sat up and blinked around, a sick daze blurring his eyes. He passed a hand over his face, shook his head again, then tried to struggle to his feet, while Len Hobart watched, emotionless and without expression.

After several false starts, Larribee finally managed to pull himself erect and weave an unsteady way over to the water seep among the aspens. In the past, some ambitious soul had dug a sizable basin for the spring and lined it with rocks. Now, on hands and knees, Jim Larribee ducked his face and head into this container of icy wetness.

The impact knocked the breath out of him, but when he got to his feet again he was fairly steady. He mopped most of the wetness from his head and face with his bandanna and came back to the buckboard. He faced Len Hobart and spoke gravely.

"They had me down and where they wanted me. They could have kicked my brains out, and were the sort to do it. But they didn't. So it must have been you who wouldn't let them?"

Len Hobart, taking a deep drag on his cigarette, shrugged. There was no friendliness in him. Larribee tried again.

"Yes, it must have been so. Thanks!" He held out his hand.

Len Hobart ignored it, while looking him bleakly in the eye.

"Larribee, you're just too damned close to Big Dan Sharples to suit me. He owns you and he owns the star you wear. If I kept Gentry and Samuels off you just now, it was because I wouldn't stand to see a dog being stomped or kicked around while helpless. So you understand how it was and how it is. Now, as long as you don't need the buckboard any more, I'm taking it home like the boss told me to."

The weakness occasioned by the beating he had taken had laid a bleak pallor across Jim Larribee's face. But under the scald of Len Hobart's blunt manner and words, deepening color again burned in his drawn cheeks. He loosed the lead rope of the buckskin, and without further look or word,

Len Hobart climbed into the buckboard and drove off.

For some time Larribee stood deep-sunk in somber thought, smarting under Len Hobart's undisguised scorn, knowing a sick, gray rage at his own blundering. Painfully he reviewed the facts.

Because of a careless moment he'd lost a prisoner and absorbed a wicked beating. On top of that, the very man who had saved him from worse abuse had refused to shake his hand or accept his thanks. Jim Larribee wasn't sure which incident carried the worst punishment.

Every instinct in him urged him to get into his saddle and run Fitch Gentry down again. But even as he would have made the first move toward doing this, the world about him went crazy again, whirling and tipping, and he had to drop to one knee to keep from spilling flat.

Common sense took over. Going after Fitch Gentry was something for the future. So, too, an understanding with Boardy Samuels. Any attempt just now at sustained or violent physical effort would be sheer stupidity. For his head was full of aching thunder, there was a draining weakness under his belt buckle, and his legs were rubbery and uncertain. He'd have enough to manage, just getting himself to town.

On all sides day was swelling full and strong, the crest of the Sabine Hills ablaze with the fire of a rising sun. Waiting until the world settled once more to a reasonable steadiness, Larribee got slowly to his feet.

His battered, trampled hat lay nearby. He cuffed this into shape and settled it gingerly on his clubbed head. His gun lay where he had dropped it, and he recovered that too. After which he tightened the cinch of his saddle, climbed painfully astride and reined the buckskin over to the road. Here sun's first long, flashing ray sliced across the world and struck warmly between his shoulders just before the timber shadows took him in.

Two hours later he splashed across the shallows east of town and rode into Silver Ford along River Street as far as Abe Chain's livery barn. Abe, small and ever curious, stared at Larribee's face as he took over the buckskin's rein.

"Jim, you been in trouble?"

Larribee grinned crookedly. "Call it so." He gave the buckskin a parting pat on the shoulder. "Plenty feed for this feller, Abe. He's earned it."

He went quickly away, then, to find rest against the sick, grinding fatigue that rode him so heavily, and also to get clear of Abe Chain's well-meant, but overly solicitous curiosity.

He went along to Valley Street, turning north there. Passing the Maverick Bar he hesitated, feeling that he could use a really stiff jolt of whisky. Then he shook his head and went on. If he stopped at the Maverick, he was sure to meet up with the same thing he'd wanted none of from Abe Chain—questions and talk.

Toward the upper end of town and set back a little from the street stood Hannah Virgil's cottage. A split picket fence enclosed it and the gate of this opened between a pair of towering poplar trees. Ever since setting up steady residence in town, Jim Larribee had roomed at Hannah Virgil's. His was a corner room with an outside door. This he never locked, and he went through it now into neatness and simplicity and a precious quiet.

There was a pitcher of water and a washbowl on a corner stand. Larribee tipped the pitcher, drank deep, then filled the bowl, stripped off his shirt and had a good wash, working gingerly around his head and face with both soap and water and with the toweling that followed.

Done with this, he pulled off his boots and stretched out on the bed to consider events just past, and what could lie in the future. These were nagging thoughts, full of the burn of frustration, but in spite of their insistence they were soon pushed aside by the demands of the physical, and sleep moved in.

He awoke to the smell of cigar smoke. The room was full of the dusky shadows of late afternoon, and, in a chair yonder, Grant Hilliker sat, a perfecto jutting at an upward tilt from his lips. This he removed, while speaking drily.

"My friend, you snore. Did you know that?"

Larribee pushed up on one elbow, blinking. His head felt heavy, but the punishing ache was gone. He rubbed a hand across his eyes, yawned, then grimaced quickly as the yawn stretched bruised and stiffened facial muscles, stirring up a twinge of pain. He swung his feet to the floor and sat on the edge of the bed.

"Must have slept pretty sound," he admitted.

"You were dead to the world," Hilliker told him. "You feel any better than you look?"

"I feel pretty good."

"What happened? Or isn't it any of my business?"

Larribee considered soberly while he lifted his shirt off the corner post of the bed, got tobacco and papers from a pocket and built a smoke.

"Nothing secret about it, I guess. The word will get around fast enough."

He drew a deep inhale, then went on to tell of his capture and subsequent loss of Fitch Gentry.

"I played it stupid," he ended bleakly. "But it's something that isn't done with by any means. In the future, I neither trust or take the word of a Gentry on anything."

"Fine!" applauded Hilliker. "Now if you'll just begin doubting the word and purposes of somebody else . . ."

"Whoa up!" Larribee was curt. "I know what

you're going to say, Grant, and I don't care to listen. Dan Sharples is all right."

"No!" argued Hilliker steadily. "He's not all right. He's a man full of dark purposes, wielding influence that's a curse across the fair face of the Pride River Valley!"

"I said: stop it!" Larribee's voice rang harshly as he got to his feet. "The man is my friend, and I won't stand for you or anybody else rawhiding him."

He took a short turn up and down the room, before squaring around to face Hilliker fully.

"When I settled on Concho Creek, who staked me to a winter's grub? Dan Sharples. When John Fredericks and Tasker Gentry got together and ran me off Concho Creek, who gave a damn? Dan Sharples."

Larribee caught up his shirt, began donning it. His tone ran a little quieter.

"It was Dan Sharples who talked me into running for sheriff against Boardy Samuels. When I did, he backed me full out, and his backing put me in office. Big Dan Sharples made it possible for me to wear—this!" Larribee touched the star on his shirt.

"That's right," agreed Grant Hilliker sardonically. "Big Dan did all you say. And now brags openly that he owns the star and owns you!"

Larribee, physically sore, depressed by the day's frustrations and stung with the stirred up emotions of the moment, flared with unthinking anger.

"That's a lie!"

Grant Hilliker's face first crimsoned, then slowly paled. He turned his back and stared out the window. When he spoke, his voice was very low.

"Jim, I'm going to let that pass, this time. But while I'm at it, I'll have my say. After which I'll close my mouth, and let you go your own way. Last evening, this happened. Big Dan Sharples stopped me and told me to stay away from you—to quit trying to put ideas in your head. Because, he bragged, you were his man."

Hilliker swung around, a cold blaze in his eyes.

"That's exactly what he said. That you were his man. That he'd made you, put the star on you and that you belonged to him. He said all that, and he threatened me and warned me off. And I told him to go to hell!"

Hilliker pointed to Larribee's star.

"Proud of that? You should be. Any man privileged to wear the authority of law should be proud of it. Providing, of course, that he keep it clean. It happens that I hold the concept of honest law with a deep and abiding respect. Feeling as I do, I despise anyone who misuses the integrity of the law, and the integrity of other men, to his own benefit. In my own small way, I'll fight such a man to my last breath!"

Grant Hilliker's cigar had gone out. Searching for a match, he gave a mirthless, faintly apologetic laugh.

"Excuse the forensics, but sometimes I get carried away by the sheer splendor of the theory of law, and when I do I go overboard."

He got his cigar going again and spoke through the pale drift of smoke.

"I agree, Jim, when you say Big Dan has done much for you. But it's when you ask yourself why he did these things that a pattern begins to form. Answer me this. When you settled on Concho Creek, was the location entirely your own choice?"

Larribee crumpled the dead stub of his cigarette between his fingers and dropped the residue in a saucer on the stand beside his bed. Then he made slow, frowning admission.

"I was new to the valley and looking for advice. Big Dan suggested Concho Creek."

"Exactly!" exclaimed Hilliker triumphantly. "And though you were brand new to this valley, though until you came riding in from the high desert and across the Sabines, he'd never laid eyes on you or knew you existed, Dan Sharples immediately trusts you for a winter's grub. Why?"

Larribee swung his shoulders restlessly.

"How would I know? Maybe he liked my honest face. For that matter, it's common knowledge that at one time or another Big Dan has carried plenty of people on his books and still does; little ranchers from the hills and grangers from the settlements downriver around Ten Mile and farther on."

"Just so," agreed Hilliker drily. "Thereby controlling the vote and political power of the valley. The vote that elects such as the county commissioners and the sheriff, and so the law of the valley. Which, my friend, is the one and only reason for any largess on the part of Big Dan Sharples."

"You don't like the man," Larribee growled, "so you see no good in him at all."

"My personal feelings toward Big Dan have nothing to do with it," said Hilliker. "I make my case on the basis of logic, on the evidence of what I see and hear. Let's consider Ira Redstone and Bert Carter. As county commissioners, they're supposed to represent the interests of all the people. Yet, let Big Dan whistle or snap his fingers and they wag their tails and roll over. Jim, have a care that Big Dan Sharples doesn't make you into something like Redstone or Carter."

Larribee shifted uneasily. "Suppose these things you're saying are true. What would Big Dan be after?"

"Not what, but who, as I see it," Hilliker said. "At a specific guess, John Fredericks. To a lesser degree, perhaps Tasker Gentry, because old Tasker has been Fredericks' friend. But John Fredericks, certainly. I've seen Big Dan Sharples look at John Fredericks, seen the dark and wicked glitter that shows in his eyes when he does so. I'm convinced that there is nothing in the world Dan Sharples would rather see than John Fredericks broken and dead at his feet."

Again Larribee's tone went harsh.

"Grant, that's damned strong talk, which I don't like. I know Big Dan has no use for John Fredericks. For that matter, after the part he had in running me off Concho Creek, I could find cause to quarrel with the man myself. But that doesn't mean I'd like to see Fredericks dead."

"You," reminded Hilliker, "are a far different breed than Big Dan Sharples. For which—God be praised! But suppose we get back to Concho Creek, which has a new settler living in the cabin you built, on the very piece of range you once hoped would be yours. None other than Mister Ed Forbush, known by everyone as another of Big Dan's trained seals."

The news jarred Jim Larribee. He stared at Hilliker narrowly. "Sure of that?"

"Quite. And you know what John Fredericks and Tasker Gentry will do about it?"

"Of course. Raise hell."

"In big and violent chunks. Forbush will set up a righteous howl for the law to protect him. Which, my friend, means you. So you'll be right where Big Dan Sharples has wanted and figured you to be, right from the first. His man, dragging his chestnuts out of the coals. Now, tell me again I'm a liar!"

"I didn't mean that and you know it," Larribee retorted gruffly. "I spoke without thinking and take it back. But Grant, you're wrong when you say Big Dan owns me. Not he or any other man owns me. He's my friend, but he doesn't own me and he never will."

Hilliker put a long, searching glance on Larribee, then nodded and moved to the door.

"That, Jim, I'm happy to hear. For the rest, one day you'll find that Dan Sharples is anything but your good friend. That day will be the first time you seriously disagree with him. Now I'll get out of your hair. Just to prove I'm still your friend—a real one—I'll buy you a drink next time we're in the Maverick."

Saying which, Grant Hilliker went away.

Alone, Jim Larribee built a fresh cigarette and smoked it to a stub as he prowled the room, restless under the tide of conjecture stirred up by Hilliker's words, and uncomfortable under the weight of it.

In less than twenty-four hours past, three different men had, in effect, laid the same brand on him. That he was Big Dan's man. That Big Dan owned him—and his star.

Fitch Gentry, at Soldier Creek. Then Len

Hobart, back in the hills. Now, right in this room, Grant Hilliker had said flatly that Big Dan was openly bragging the fact. This last was the real sticker.

You might, mused Larribee somberly, write off the statements of Fitch Gentry and Len Hobart as product of varying degrees of hostility. But you couldn't as casually brush aside Hilliker's disclosures. Grant Hilliker had come as a friend, and was a man of unquestioned integrity. His word was good.

Larribee came to the window of his room, paused there in his restless pacing, stared out into the warm tide of the lengthening afternoon. Abruptly he sharpened to alertness, watching. Over at a far corner of the yard, beyond a thin hedge of lilac bushes, there was movement, furtive movement, which resolved into the thin, waspy figure of Dobe Lear. Dobe, half crouched, got clear of the yard, then broke down toward the river and out of sight.

Jim Larribee stood motionless, a hard and wary anger deepening in his eyes. He rubbed a hand across his chin and along the angle of his jaw, the whisker stubble making a harsh rasp under his palm. A shave was in order and would make him feel better. After that, certain people were going to be set right on several things. . . .

He took the pitcher from the washstand and

headed for Hannah Virgil's kitchen after hot water.

Five minutes later, in the alley between the back wall of the Maverick Bar and the side wall of Cap Porter's saddle shop, Dobe Lear moved cautiously along until he could make a careful survey of River Street, before stepping out into it: which was ever his way.

For this waspy little man was slave to the habit of a deep-seated furtiveness. He was as wary as a wolf, sly as a fox. He prowled and looked and listened, filled always with a blank venom which some inner twist brewed and kept renewed in him. Beyond personal concern, he owned to but one allegiance, which was to Big Dan Sharples. Other than that, not knowing the real meaning of trust himself, he trusted no one.

Having had his full, careful look at River Street, Dobe went along it, holding closely to the side wall of the Maverick Bar on his right. Even in the open, he seemed to slink. Reaching the corner of River Street and Valley, he paused for another look around.

A granger from Ten Mile had his wagon drawn up in front of the Acme Mercantile, and Big Dan stood on the porch, talking to the man. Dobe waited until this talk was done and the granger gone off downstreet. Then he crossed over.

Big Dan lowered his ungainly bulk into his favorite chair, while Dobe hunkered down on his heels, back to the wall, spinning up one of his interminable, match-thin, brown-paper cigarettes. Big Dan lighted a cigar and presently grunted:

"Well?"

"Hilliker told Larribee you were braggin' you owned him and his star," Dobe reported in his droning, toneless way.

Big Dan cursed, growlingly. "I've had a big plenty of that fellow. He needs a lesson." He was silent a moment, then asked: "What did Larribee have to say?"

Dobe shrugged narrow shoulders.

"Hilliker was near the window, so I got his words pretty clear. But Larribee was deeper back in the room and I couldn't get him as well. I know there was considerable edge to his voice at first, like he was mad, maybe. Then he quieted down, like he'd been convinced of something. Boss, you ever figgered what you'd be up against, should Larribee turn stubborn and not play along?"

For some time Big Dan was silent, peering through the blue coiling smoke of his cigar with eyes hooded and dark.

"Yeah," he admitted finally, "I have. And should it happen, I got an answer for that too."

4

His face smarting pleasantly from the slide of his razor across bruised flesh, Jim Larribee stood between the framing poplar trees at the gate of Hannah Virgil's yard. The sun had dipped beyond the Maacama Rim, and now that western boundary of the Pride River Valley lay drowned in a powder-blue sea of softened color, the sweep of this shadow already reaching town and beginning to envelope it. Overhead, in the poplars, some sparrows were fussing and twittering, while from its perch on a dead willow snag down by the river, a mourning dove sobbed its melancholy plaint.

The few hours of sleep he'd managed had done a lot for Larribee. His head was sore but clear, and much of the stiffness had worked out of his beaten muscles. When he moved off downstreet, the old, smooth vigor was back in his stride.

He crossed Valley Street, climbed to the porch of the Acme Mercantile, and turned in at the wide door. Old Charley Clark was alone in the vast gloom of the place and, at Larribee's question, jerked his head toward the rear.

Larribee let himself into Big Dan's living quarters, and was met by a tide of savory supper odors. It was Big Dan himself who was busy over the stove, where a griddle of ham sizzled and a pot of coffee steamed and chuckled. A lamp burned on the table and, hunkered on his heels in a half-shadowed corner, Dobe Lear sucked on a cigarette.

At Larribee's entrance, Big Dan turned and exclaimed heartily:

"Jim! Just in time. How'd a supper of ham and eggs go?"

Larribee hesitated. "I didn't come in with the idea of sponging a meal."

Big Dan waved a careless hand. "What the hell! I got a whole warehouse full of grub. Dobe, the woodbox needs another arm of wood."

Dobe got to his feet and went out the back door. Big Dan laid a solid glance on Larribee, an edge of heaviness deepening his tone.

"You went out after Fitch Gentry. You come back without him, showing signs of rough handling. What happened?"

"I caught up with him at Soldier Creek and brought him back as far as Sweetwater Glade. I turned a little careless there, and with Boardy Samuels helping him, he got clear."

"You were careless—how?"

The weight and pressing insistence behind Big Dan's questions started a burn of color in Larribee's face. But he kept his tone even as he explained.

"I turned my back on Fitch while I argued with

Boardy Samuels. I had Fitch handcuffed and figured him harmless that way. He wasn't. He jumped me from behind and slugged me with the handcuffs. Then Boardy bought in. Between the two of them—well—"

Big Dan grunted sarcastically. "When are you going to learn! Any time you turn your back on a Gentry or a Fredericks, you'll always get slugged. Did old Hack Gregg tell it right—the Fredericks girl was hauling Fitch out to Soldier Creek by buckboard?"

"That's the way it was," Larribee admitted briefly. "But there's no point in making talk about it. Being some on the headstrong side, Kelsey Fredericks was just acting on impulse."

"Impulse, be damned!" exploded Big Dan harshly. "Don't be so gullible. It's high time you were getting smart where those two tribes are concerned. Have you ever had any other treatment but the wrong kind from a Fredericks or a Gentry? They ran you off Concho Creek, didn't they?"

"Call it that. Speaking of Concho Creek, I understand you got Ed Forbush up there. What's the point, Dan? You know it will stir up trouble."

Big Dan turned back to the stove, and spoke across his shoulder.

"Forbush has every legal right to settle on Concho Creek. And neither John Fredericks or Tasker Gentry got the right to run him off. But they're certain to try. So you ride up there first thing in the morning and see that everything is quiet."

Jim Larribee studied the ungainly figure before him. The bulging, ponderous body on the long, almost stiltlike legs. The heavy head with its roach of coarse roan hair. Dismal conviction came to Jim Larribee. Here it was—the thing Grant Hilliker had said. And Fitch Gentry and Len Hobart—

For in Big Dan's words had been a flat order.

Big Dan's man, not his own. Big Dan, not he, ordering the working of the star. Just another of Big Dan's puppets, like Dobe Lear yonder, now coming in the back door with an armful of wood. Bark and roll over whenever Big Dan snapped the whip. That was what Big Dan figured he added up to. . . .

Stirring anger harshened Larribee's words.

"I'm going to ride up to Concho Creek, Dan—for one reason. Not to back Forbush's hand, but to tell him to get the hell out of there—and see that he does!"

Big Dan came around as though stung with a hot iron. "You'll—what? You'd order Forbush off Concho Creek?"

"Just so! You speak of legal rights. If any such exist on that stream, they're mine. For I put in exactly five months and twenty-seven days on Concho Creek. I built a cabin there with my own two hands. I sunk considerable work and hardship into that place. And I don't know of anybody else who did. So, if anyone has a legitimate claim there, I have. And I'm not letting some hard-case boomer like Ed Forbush move in and take over—let alone help him do it!"

Big Dan's eyes pinched back until they seemed almost hidden behind the hooded lids, and there was the cold cut of acid in his voice.

"When Fitch Gentry hit you that clout on the head, he must have knocked you loose from your senses. I say this once more. Ed Forbush is on Concho Creek and entitled to the protection of the law to see he stays there. You give him that protection!"

Here, thought Larribee grimly, it was. For better or worse, here it was. He shrugged.

"Dan, I've felt that you were my good friend. One way or another, you've done a lot of things for me. I've been grateful for favors done. Now I'm wondering if you did these things purely as a friend, with no thought of anything in return except friendship, or whether it's been all just part of a program aimed at making me into something you could use to further some scheme of your own. I want a straight answer, Dan—And I want it now!"

He didn't get it. Big Dan turned back to the stove and spoke as though to himself.

"You grubstake a man and give him advice.

When he gets knocked down, you pick him up and put some fight back into him. You back him for sheriff and you get him elected. You do these things for him when nobody else gives a thin damn whether he lives or dies or what happens to him. After all that, he questions your friendship . . ."

It had a high sound, but it didn't ring true.

"You did all those things, Dan," Larribee said. "But that isn't the direct answer I asked for."

Big Dan came around again. There was something almost ursine in the way his coarse nostrils flared.

"Tired of this," he said thickly. "Goddamn tired of it! I bid for a man's friendship only once. Then—to hell with him! Next move is yours, Larribee."

Larribee marked him with a still, cold glance, then nodded.

"Fair enough, Dan. People have begun to wonder just who really wears the star in this valley. I'm clearing the record on that point. I'm wearing it—Jim Larribee! And—nobody else! I'm playing no favorites. As sheriff, my job is to stop trouble. Easiest way to stop it is to head it off before it starts. So, Ed Forbush gets off Concho Creek. Now, while I'm having my say, here's something else I want damn' well understood. I won't stand being spied on!"

Larribee turned and put his glance on Dobe

Lear, who had just dumped his armful of wood into the box at the end of the stove.

"Dobe, don't you ever prowl Hannah Virgil's yard again! If you have legitimate business with Mrs. Virgil or me, you come in the front gate like a man and knock at a door. I see you sneaking again, I'll figure you're up to no good and I'll make you damned hard to catch!"

Dobe went still, slightly crouched, eyes filming with a startled malevolence. Then, wordless, he sidled over to the wall and hunkered down, just as he had been when Larribee first entered the room.

Once more Big Dan turned to the stove. He spoke with an attempt at heartiness, but it wasn't very convincing, for his voice was still thick with anger.

"Where's the sense to this fool arguing? Everybody's hungry, everybody's edgy. Let's eat and quit the fussing."

Jim Larribee shook his head. "Thanks, Dan. Not tonight."

The moment the door fully closed behind Larribee, Dobe Lear began cursing with a thin wickedness. Big Dan stopped him bluntly.

"Shut up! That does no good. You must have been careless, letting him spot you in that yard."

Dobe's shrug was small and sulky. "I did my best."

This would be true enough. To the limit of his

ability, Dobe was faithful. Nor would railing or cursing or accusations, one way or another, be of any help. Here, Big Dan realized, was something that called for cold and realistic reasoning.

He slid ham and eggs on to a platter and motioned Dobe up to the table. Dobe, relaxing a little, said:

"Larribee's got away from us, boss. That damned lawyer, Hilliker, he's turned Larribee against us."

Big Dan brooded for a little time.

"We'll see," he growled, "we'll see."

Directly across Valley Street from the Riverside Hotel was the White Stag eating house. Jim Larribee took supper there, before going on down Valley to his office. In between the White Stag and the office was the small laundry establishment of the Rojas family: of Ysidro Rojas, his wife Maria, and Rita, a sixteen-year-old daughter. As Larribee passed the place he heard the strumming of Ysidro's guitar, and a fragment of a Mexican folk song in Maria's full, soft voice.

For a moment he paused, knowing vague envy. These people, he thought, knew how to live. Frugal and hard working and in no way cursed with great ambitions, they were content with the simple goodness of life which their small business allowed them. They had no enemies, no great problems. Ysidro was a wiry, quick-moving man, Maria buxom and deliberate, and Rita full of youth's vital grace and beauty. Larribee was fond of the entire family.

In his office he got a light going, then settled down with his after-supper cigarette and his thoughts. There was scant comfort in the latter. Back in Big Dan's quarters, things had been dangerously close to an open break, and this he did not want: for he valued Big Dan's friendship. But, he told himself grimly, it had to come to him with no strings attached.

Movement at the office door became Rita Rojas, whirling in with a flutter of skirts, the gleam of white teeth and the sparkle of dark eyes.

"Jeem! W'ere you be so long? W'y you look like—like—?"

She paused in her breathless girlish chatter, her eyes widening as she noted the staining bruises on his face, his cut and swollen lips. She circled the desk swiftly, leaned against his shoulder, her fingers running lightly over bruise and cut. Abruptly she flared.

"Who do this to you? I scratch their eyes out!"

She pressed closer, crooning sympathy, as softly warm and affectionate as a kitten. She would have put an arm about his neck but he warded her off gently, smiling.

"Now—now! Behave yourself, young 'un, or I'll turn you over my knee."

In no way dismayed, she perched on a corner of the desk, swinging her feet, eying him with mock reproach.

"You do not love me any more," she accused. "So maybe I will not love you. W'at you think of that, Jeem Larribee?"

His smile widened. "I think you're a little devil, trying to grow up too fast. And as your big brother, I may have to take steps and wallop you."

"Big brother!" She made a face, sniffed. "I do not want a big brother. I want a sweetheart. So, I think I will love you anyway, even if you do not love me."

Now she sobered and quit her teasing, her dark eyes searching his face. She leaned over and again touched the bruise along his jaw.

"This. It hurts, Jeem—no?"

"A little. It's my feelings that are really damaged. I'm tired and full of troubles, young 'un."

"W'y you so?"

"No man enjoys being played for a fool. I think I have."

She considered this for a moment. Then she gave her shoulders an indignant twist.

"But you are not a fool. Anybody say so, I hate them." Then, with startling perception for one of sixteen, "W'at I think, Jeem, is you are sometimes lonely?"

He met her eyes and nodded slowly. "Sometimes. And when I am you seem to understand and come to cheer me up. You're a sweet youngster, Rita."

She fairly wriggled with delight. "W'en you talk nice things like that, Jeem, I love you more."

"Maybe," he suggested, gently dry, "you should save some of that love for young Henry Jeffers."

Startled color swept up her brown young throat and through her dusky cheeks. She tossed her head.

"Hennery Jeffers!" The name rolled off her tongue in liquid cadence. "W'at I care for Hennery Jeffers? He is a great—great ox."

"Henry's a good boy," Larribee said. "Honest, hard working, knows where he is going." Smiling, he added, "Oh, he's big, all right. Big enough to keep the likes of you from kicking over the traces."

She made another face. "I can wind Hennery Jeffers around my littlest finger." An imp of deviltry shone in her eyes and she giggled. "I do it too. W'en I speak to him and smile at him, then he is all red, and there is no place for his hands and feet." She chortled at the memory, then softly added, "He is nice—so nice."

Larribee eyed her skeptically.

"Sometimes I think you are like a sparrow in a poplar tree, empty-headed and full of nothing but chatter and flutter. Again, like now, I'm not so sure."

A mutter of hoofs sounded along the street, coming to a stop at the rail beyond the office door. Saddle gear creaked as a rider dismounted. Larribee tipped a dismissing head.

"Scat, my little one!"

Rita darted for the door, barely missed colliding with John Fredericks as he entered.

"Whoa up, young lady!" exclaimed the cattleman gruffly, but not unkindly. "Don't stomp me under."

Rita gave him a dazzling smile and was gone.

John Fredericks had a coat over his arm. He laid it on the desk.

"Yours," he said briefly. "Kelsey asked me to leave it and to thank you for its use."

Larribee nodded. "Glad it helped out."

"I'm adding my thanks for your consideration of her," Fredericks said. "Under the conditions, it was pretty decent of you." He hesitated, then added, "Len Hobart told me how things came out between you and Fitch Gentry at Sweetwater Glade, after I left. I was sorry to hear it."

Jim Larribee leaned forward, meeting John Fredericks' stern, deep-set glance.

"You mean that?"

"Certainly. I've never had any illusions about Fitch Gentry. He's no damned good. I've tolerated him for the sake of his father, my good friend and neighbor, and a hundred times the man his son will ever be. Through his damned whining around, Fitch talked my daughter into making a sizable fool of herself, and that finishes him with me, finally and for good. Should you put him behind bars for good and all, it's all right with me. You may have wondered why Kelsey consented to drive him out to the stage station at Soldier Creek?"

"I've wondered," admitted Larribee. "I think, like I said at Sweetwater Glade, it was just a headlong, generous impulse."

"Partly so. More particularly, the feeling that in helping Fitch pull a run-out, she was striking a blow at Big Dan Sharples. And," Fredericks added, with some dryness, "where my enemies are concerned, Kelsey is a very partisan daughter."

"Fitch Gentry," Larribee reminded, "was my prisoner, and that of no other man. Why should anyone think different?"

"Because," John Fredericks said, laying the words down bluntly, "the general opinion up and down this valley is that you and your star answer pretty much to the orders of Big Dan Sharples."

Badgered anger quickened in Jim Larribee. Here it was again. He got to his feet, so he could meet the cattleman's eyes on a penetrating level.

"You mean," he said, "like the star answered

to you and Tasker Gentry when Boardy Samuels was wearing it?"

Fredericks flushed slightly.

"Sometimes, in sheer self-defense, a man uses any cards he can lay hold of. He may not be proud of them, but he uses them because he has to."

"Very well," came back Larribee. "Maybe, having had the example set, that's the way Dan Sharples feels. If he does, who has the right to blame him?"

"That," John Fredericks said coldly, "could depend on where you stand when you look at Big Dan Sharples. You, apparently, stand in one place, while I stand in another." Saying such, the cattleman turned to leave.

Larribee stopped him with an upraised hand.

"A minute. This, I want you to hear. I want you to hear it and carry the word with you and spread it as you go. Which is, that while I wear this star, it plays no favorites. Not you, not Dan Sharples, not anybody. It is not now, hasn't been, isn't going to be influenced by money, friendship, enmity, threat or promise. You can believe that, even if it does sound very righteous!"

The cattleman studied him, glance reserved and skeptical. "Have you said as much to Dan Sharples?"

"I have. I don't know the true cause of the bad blood between you and Dan Sharples, and I don't know where the real right and wrong of it lies. This, however, I'm sure of. I'm in the middle! It could turn into a damned lonely spot. Well, that's all right with me; the middle is where I stay, playing no favorites. And anybody who sets out to use me for a sucker or handy man, will damn well learn some of the hard facts of life!"

John Fredericks stood for some little time, showing that same guarded skepticism. Then he shrugged.

"I'm willing to be convinced, Larribee."

With that, he moved on into the night.

From Larribee's office, John Fredericks made the short ride up Valley and across River Street to the hitch rail in front of the Maverick Bar. Here he dismounted and tied, but instead of going into the Maverick, as had been his first intent, he paused for a little time, his glance fixed on the long, sprawling front of the Acme Mercantile across the street.

Over there, in the deep gloom cast by the overhang of the porch gallery, he saw the crimson eye of a cigar tip wink bright, fade, then wink bright again. He knew who would be smoking that cigar, and abrupt decision sent him tramping through the street's dust. He climbed to the store porch, then paused as Big Dan Sharples' voice hit roughly out.

"Far enough, Fredericks! There's nothing here for you. You should know that."

"Dan," Fredericks said quietly, "you got good eyes. Too bad they don't see as clearly in all things."

"I see enough," came the harsh retort. "I don't need eyes to recognize you."

"What you mean is, if you hate a man enough, you can feel his presence?"

"That's it! Get off my property!"

"Presently, presently! I came over here to have my say on a couple of matters, and I'm going to have it. First, get rid of that sneaking little whelp hunkered down by your chair." The cattleman's tone took on a whiplash bite. "Go on, Lear. Get the hell out of here while I talk with your master!"

"No!" blurted Big Dan, lunging half out of his chair. "Dobe stays put! He's my man, and answers only to me."

"A mistake you keep making, Dan," observed Fredericks. "Claiming this man and that, as yours, as if they were dogs and you owned them, inside and out. That might be true with some, but not all. When they do turn up dogs, then they're fit only to be kicked around. Like now. Lear, I'm not telling you again. Get out of here!"

Dobe Lear came to his feet, small and twisted and hating, but cowed by the power and authority in Fredericks' words and manner.

"By God!" raged Big Dan, "I got a notion to tell Dobe to—!"

"Don't!" Fredericks cut in bluntly. "By this time, Dan, you should know you don't scare me. Now I'm here for just one reason; a final, serious talk between the two of us. Some of the things we may say won't be for the ears of such as this slinking little rat. Get rid of him!"

Big Dan's heavy teeth set down on his cigar so savagely he bit it clean in half. He threw the mangled butt out into the street's dust, spat the tattered, bitter dregs after it. Baffled and thwarted by the cool, flat defiance of John Fredericks, he knew a frustrated fury.

Many a time had he visualized John Fredericks dead at his feet, and had reveled in that dark fancy. Right now there was nothing he wanted to do more than to call on Dobe Lear to throw a gun and turn the fancy into fact. But the words strangled in his throat; for this was neither time or place for such decision. He settled back in his chair and his words ran heavy.

"All right, Dobe. Come back in half an hour."

Dobe drifted along the porch, dropped off into the street and was lost in its darkness.

There was another chair and John Fredericks dragged it up, sat down, stoked a pipe and lighted it.

"Dan, you're wondering why I'm here. I'll tell you. It's for a final try at peace. It strikes me that hate, if a man hangs on to it long enough, can turn pretty pointless. Certainly these years of it haven't done either of us any good. What say we call it quits?"

Big Dan cleared his throat.

"Turning mealy mouthed is the last thing I expected of you, Fredericks. What's the real truth? You scared of the cards I hold?"

"You don't hold a single card that scares me," retorted Fredericks. "My reasoning runs like this. When a man's young, he can know a sort of brute pride in batting heads with anyone he figures is trying to challenge him. He might even find a certain satisfaction in it. Makes him feel he's wide across the shoulders and deep through the chest. Also," drily, "it could prove that he still lacks a full measure of good sense."

The cattleman paused to run another match across the bowl of his pipe.

"Tonight, Dan, I'm thinking back to when the two of us first came to the Pride River Valley, riding the same Butterfield mud wagon, when the name Silver Ford meant a single building and a corral, no more. We had an even hundred dollars between us. We split it, fifty fifty. Your bent was trading, mine cattle. We both started with little more than a big idea, and from there we've come quite a distance. But along the trail we lost something that at one time had value, and replaced it with something worthless. We lost friendship and found enmity. We could both be the poorer for it."

Big Dan rolled the hate phlegm in his throat again.

"If there's a point, Fredericks, get to it! I tell you I'm tired of the mealy mouth."

John Fredericks stared at the dark, formless blob in the chair beside him. Then he spoke softly, half musing.

"You've hated too long and too well, Dan. It's blinded you completely to reason and common sense. Very well, I'll make no more talk about peace. I'll just toss a few facts at you and then go my way. The day your hate for me really started was the day Lutie Hammond and I were married. Right?"

In his chair, Big Dan Sharples caught his breath, then went utterly still.

"Lutie Hammond!" John Fredericks handled the name with a reverent gentleness. "How bright and lovely she was! And—she married me. She had that right, Dan—to marry the man of her choice. But the day she did, you went off on a drunk that lasted weeks. Somewhere along the course of that drunk, you reached way down in some dark hell and came up with your big hate for me. Maybe for Lutie too. I've wondered, had Lutie lived, if you'd have fought the two of us the way you've fought me . . . ?

"Well, I walked across the street tonight to try a final appeal to reason. I came to suggest that we stop right where we are, and that we live and let live. I see now it was a useless hope."

Fredericks stood up and moved along to the top of the porch steps. There he paused and spoke again, his voice taking on a harsh, ringing note.

"I'm giving you a week—no more—to get Ed Forbush off Concho Creek. If he isn't gone in that time, then I run him off—rough. Even if I have to kill him! And if my hand is forced that far, I'll know there can never be any peace for me in this world until you're dead too. So, I'll come after you. Better think on it, Dan!"

Dan Sharples, watching, lost John Fredericks in the street's gloom, then picked up the spare, erect figure again as Fredericks pushed through the doors of the Maverick. Here, he told himself savagely, was another thing he hated about John Fredericks. It was the easy way Fredericks moved among other men, and the respect men showed him. Over there in the Maverick Bar, men would invite John Fredericks to drink with them, would be flattered should he accept, and even more so should he invite them to drink with him.

It had been a long time since Dan Sharples had been in the Maverick, and he couldn't remember when other men had invited him to drink with them. The habit had come to him of drinking alone. He felt the need of a drink now, and, leaving the store porch, he went back through the darkness to his living quarters, picking an unerring way, even without a light.

He didn't bother with a glass, just tipped the bottle at his lips and gulped, long and deep. He put the bottle away and went back out on the porch and found his usual chair. The fire of the whisky burned in his belly, and his thoughts began to quicken and enlarge. By the time Dobe Lear came slipping back out of the night to his regular spot beside Big Dan's chair, Big Dan was drawing on a fresh cigar and had his moves figured. He held his voice to a growling murmur.

"Dobe, I want you to locate Boardy Samuels."

Dobe, startled, paused in the building of a cigarette.

"Boardy Samuels! What you want with him?"

"A talk. Tell him to come see me—on the quiet."

"May take me a little time to catch him alone," Dobe said. "And mebbe he won't come for a talk with you. He ain't your man, boss."

"He'll come," Big Dan said. "Just ask him how he'd like to be sheriff again. That'll bring him."

"Hah!" grunted Dobe, the implication of these words jerking him erect. "When you want him?"

"As soon as possible. You might as well pull out tonight. Along your way, stop at Concho Creek and tell Curly Gibson to come on in. I got a chore for him too."

"Boss," said Dobe, "you're up to something. What?"

"Never mind," answered Big Dan. "You go get Samuels."

5

Born of three never-failing, strong-flowing springs well up in the rugged Maacama Rim country, Concho Creek fought a foaming, tumultuous way down rocky gorge and gulch for a full two miles before making a final sheer sixty-foot leap into a boiling, fern-lined pool. From this point on it turned sleepy and soft-voiced, sliding along over shining gravel, under cool, shadowy tunnels of willow and alder, through steadily widening meadows bracketed north and south by low ridges sprawling fanwise from the rim. These ridges steadily rounded and flattened as they ran, gradually losing themselves in the general sweep of the big valley of the Pride River. Across this flatness, Concho Creek meandered to finally find confluence with the river.

The cabin Jim Larribee had built stood at the edge of an alder grove, some hundred yards downcreek from the falls. Now, through the cool, moist dawn, Larribee rode up to it, the sound of his approach first muffled by the meadow grass, then completely muted by the voice of the falls. Woodsmoke was a thin, blue drift above the cabin chimney, and in the pole-corral yonder, three horses lifted their heads and watched him, prick-eared.

Larribee stepped down, dropped his reins, and his horse, dragging these, immediately moved over to the corral to commune across the top rail with its fellows. Beside the cabin door was a bench holding a bucket of water, a tin basin and a piece of soap in a can. From a nail above the bench hung a limp towel that had already seen considerable use. Now the cabin door opened and it was Curly Gibson who came out, yawning, turning toward the washbench, then going still and watchful as he glimpsed Larribee.

"Go ahead, Curly," Larribee drawled. "Wash your face. Never let it be said I stood between you and your need for soap and water."

The words, though apparently casual, carried deeper meaning than they seemed, a fact which Curly Gibson did not miss; for by habit he was an untidy, slovenly sort. He colored, scowled and prepared to wash.

Now Ed Forbush appeared in the doorway of the cabin, a high, lank man with sharp, bony features. His reddish-brown eyes were habitually suspicious and a ragged, roan-colored mustache covered his tight mouth. In almost the exact center of each narrow cheek was a small, round, puckered scar. Common talk was that these had been caused by a bullet that had passed cleanly through the man's mouth from side to side. No one knew for sure, as Forbush never spoke about his past. Now he jerked a nod at

Larribee and his words came, nasal and twanging.

"Coffee's on. Come in and drink up. Big Dan send you to see how things were? He said he was going to."

"He mentioned it last night," Larribee admitted. "But I'd have ridden in anyhow, once I heard you were here."

"How's that? Ain't been a sign of trouble from Fredericks or Gentry yet. I'm wonderin' if they even know I'm here."

"They know," said Larribee, following Forbush into the cabin.

On the stove a battered coffeepot was snoring, and Forbush poured a steaming cup for Larribee, who cradled it in both hands and sipped the scalding contents cautiously. His glance ran around the place, and every board and nailhead was familiar. They should have been, he mused bleakly, seeing he'd put them there with his own hands.

Curly Gibson came in, coarse hair dripping and roughly smoothed down. He stood at one end of the stove with his coffee, staring sourly straight ahead.

Ed Forbush, held with innate suspicion, said:

"Maybe I caught a little something extra in what you said about riding in here, whether or not Big Dan sent you. Did I?"

Larribee nodded. "I came by to tell you to roll your gear and pull out."

Forbush, pouring coffee for himself, was startled enough to miss the cup and spill some of the fluid on the hot stove top, where it crackled and bounced and set up a steamy, scorched smell.

"What the hell do you mean?" he demanded, coming sharply around. "That's not Big Dan's order?"

"No. It's mine."

Forbush laughed harshly. "Let's talk sense. It's too early in the day for a joke."

"No joke there," Larribee said, putting his cup on the table. "You heard me exactly right. Roll your gear and drift."

Forbush squared himself, feet spread, reddish brown eyes narrowly angry.

"I don't savvy. And when I don't savvy, I listen. Talk, Larribee! What's the rest of it?"

"That's all of it. I'm telling you to get out."

"Why?"

"Your staying here would surely start trouble. I head that off by removing the cause. You!"

"Then Big Dan isn't ordering this?"

"I told you he wasn't. I am."

"It's no good," said Forbush. "I take my orders from Big Dan Sharples. So do you."

"Forbush," Larribee said, dangerously soft, "are you pulling out or do I have to get rough?"

Forbush leveled a defiant, stabbing finger at Larribee's chest.

"I don't know what kind of a deal you think

you're trying to put over, but whatever it is, it don't go with me. When Big Dan tells me to pull out of here, I will. Not before. And if you're out to double cross—!"

That was as far as he got when Larribee hit him, a winging blow that slashed into the side of Forbush's narrow jaw. It spun Forbush around, sent him reeling across the cabin and dropped him, numbed and floundering, at the base of the wall.

It happened so fast Curly Gibson could do nothing but stare. His gun and belt hung on a wall peg at the head of one of the two bunks in the cabin. When, presently, he glanced that way, Larribee warned him sharply.

"Don't try it, Curly!"

Larribee cushioned the knuckles of his right hand in the palm of his left, massaging them slowly while watching Ed Forbush gather his jarred wits and climb shakily back to his feet. As the blankness cleared from Forbush's eyes, they narrowed to wicked glints, and under the ragged, roan mustache his mouth was just a thin, bitter line.

"You shouldn't have done that, Larribee," he said tonelessly. "You shouldn't have hit me."

Larribee stepped over, drew Curly's gun from the leather, flipped back the loading gate and, spinning the cylinder with his thumb, dropped the weighty loads into his hand.

“Roll your gear,” he said remorselessly. “Both of you.”

Forbush had a rifle leaning in a corner and Larribee, having unloaded Curly’s belt gun, picked up the rifle and levered it empty too.

Forbush said, “You’ll never make it stick, Larribee. You just don’t rate that big.”

“Do I have to hit you again?” Larribee asked.

Forbush cursed in a wild, helpless way and began getting his stuff together. Fifteen minutes later he and Curly Gibson rode away from the cabin, heading downcreek. Just before they left, Larribee handed their empty weapons to them.

“I wouldn’t have gone to all this trouble if I didn’t figure to make it stick,” he said. “Remember that!”

Tasker Gentry was a gaunt, leathery man, whose deep-set blue eyes burned out from under shaggy, frosted brows. The inexorable sculpture of the years, coupled to the acid of some deep inner bitterness, had seamed his face. He stood beside a corral fence at Gentry headquarters, an elbow hooked over the top rail, and he spoke harshly.

“Fitch? He ain’t here. He pulled out last night. I gave him his choice, one way or the other. And if he didn’t come to you, I don’t know where he went.”

Jim Larribee slouched in his saddle, laying

most of his weight in the near stirrup. He looked down at Tasker Gentry gravely.

"I don't think I understand," he said. "You gave Fitch his choice?"

"That's right. I told him he could head for town and give himself up to you, or he could get off the ranch and not come back until he was man enough to live up to his sworn, given word. Anybody who won't do that, ain't never going to be worth a damn, whether he's a son of mine or whoever he is. Fitch gave his word, didn't he, that he wouldn't try a runout if he was allowed to bring his bad leg home where it could be tended better? He gave his word—?"

Larribee nodded. "Yes, he did."

"Gave his word," said Tasker Gentry bleakly, staring out across the far run of the valley, "and then broke it! Yeah, broke it, just like he was no better than any other damn' brush-jumpin' no-good."

Now there came to Jim Larribee an understanding of the true nature of the inner bitterness that was helping carve those deep lines in Tasker Gentry's face. He knew a quick flicker of sympathy for the old fellow. He straightened in his saddle.

"You understand, of course, I got to go right on trying to run Fitch down. But that isn't the only reason I came by. I wanted you to know that I just ran Ed Forbush off Concho Creek."

Tasker Gentry brought his glance quickly back to Larribee's face.

"You—what! Run Forbush off Concho?"

"I did."

"Why?" rapped the old fellow bluntly. "You're supposed to be playing the same side of the trail as him. Big Dan Sharples' side."

"A lot of people have been jumping at that conclusion," Larribee said evenly. "And—they're wrong. I'm not playing either side of a trail. I'm traveling right down the middle of it."

"Why are you telling me this, Larribee?"

"So you won't go brewing war smoke. I'm telling John Fredericks the same thing. The valley is fairly quiet now. I want to keep it that way. Boardy Samuels around?"

Tasker Gentry shook a grizzled head.

"Him and the crew pulled out early this morning to work some cattle back on my bench range under the rim. They'll be three, four days at that chore, I expect. What you want Boardy for?"

"It can wait," said Larribee, lifting his reins.

Measured by the north-south compass lines of the valley, the headquarters of John Fredericks and Tasker Gentry stood about even, the Gentry layout on the west side of the river, the Fredericks range on the east, the ranch buildings of the latter dominating the bight of a mile long, crescent-shaped meadow slicing back against the base of the Sabines.

The first dwelling John Fredericks had built in the Pride River Valley was a one-room cabin, which had been enough for its original purpose, that of offering a young and savagely ambitious bachelor cattleman a place to eat and sleep. But when the worst of those toil- and hardship-whipped years lay behind him, and with a new and adored young wife to provide for, John Fredericks had built a second time, a spacious, solid ranch house that gleamed white and cool in the spaced and tapered shade of several poplar trees.

The fact that the young wife had lived but one short year to enjoy that new home had been a shattering blow to John Fredericks, but he had found comfort in raising the infant daughter left to him, a daughter who had grown to resemble so much the mother she could not remember. Time had mellowed the cattleman's loss, but memory had kept the image of his girl wife soft and warm and sure in his heart, and the rose garden Lutie Fredericks had planted in front of the ranch house had been preserved and renewed in the exact pattern she had given it.

Busy in it now, as Jim Larribee rode up, was Kelsey Fredericks. Larribee pulled in his horse at the hitch rail beside the gate in the split picket fence, looked at Kelsey and touched his hat.

"Your father?"

She faced him steadily, gravely quiet, her

cheeks warm in morning sun, her glance searching his face as though to confirm what she had heard concerning the now fading marks of conflict. She tipped her head toward the house.

"I'll call him," she said.

As she turned to do so, John Fredericks appeared on the long, deep porch that ran across the front of the house. He spoke gruffly but without hostility.

"Come on up!"

Larribee opened the gate and went along the path. Kelsey Fredericks walked ahead of him, graceful and quick in a simple blue house dress. The sun glinted on her head, ferreting out glints of dark chestnut among the soft folds of her hair. She carried several freshly cut rose blooms across the curve of her arm, and their deep fragrance drifted back to Larribee, warm and rich.

Kelsey went right on into the house with her flowers. There were several chairs on the porch, as well as a hammock swinging empty at one shaded end. John Fredericks indicated a chair to Larribee, pulled one up for himself.

"I won't bother you long," Larribee said. "I came by to tell you I moved Ed Forbush off Concho Creek this morning."

Fredericks swung a startled head. "Big Dan Sharples tell you to?"

Jim Larribee showed a turn of impatience. "I hoped I'd made it clear to you last night that

Big Dan isn't telling me what to do. Neither is anyone else."

"Then why did you do it? What reason did you have for moving Forbush off Concho?"

"You can have the same answer I gave Tasker Gentry. I moved Forbush out to head off trouble."

John Fredericks studied Larribee narrowly. "You agree, then, that Forbush was Big Dan's man, acting strictly to Big Dan's orders?"

"Yes, I do. Forbush said he intended to stay on Concho until Big Dan ordered him off." Larribee paused to spin up a smoke, then added, "I changed his mind on that point."

John Fredericks slid a little deeper in his chair, frowning.

"Larribee," he said slowly, "had I guessed you were so much your own man, you might still be holding down that little layout you started on Concho Creek. Actually, Tasker Gentry and I never did have anything directly against you personally. It was against what we thought you were."

"You figured me another Ed Forbush, digging in on Concho in Big Dan's interests, not my own?"

"That's it."

Larribee, thoughtful for a moment, asked:

"What makes Concho Creek so extra special with you and Gentry? I admit it's a pretty spot for a ranch headquarters and that it's good range on both sides of the creek clear to the river. But is it worth fighting a lifetime feud over?"

"Intrinsically, no," said Fredericks. "But for what it represents, yes. In the old days, Gentry and I ran our cattle over just about all of the valley. Then the grangers started coming in down around Ten Mile. Gentry and I had to make a decision. We could try and keep the grangers out of the valley entirely—and get tromped under doing it—or we could let the grangers have the southern end while we moved up to this end where we'd stand at least a fifty-fifty chance of holding our own.

"Now you've certainly noted that backbone of hungry land that runs east and west across the valley about halfway between town and Concho Creek? Well, no granger wants any part of it, knowing they'd starve to death quick if they tried to farm it. It isn't worth much as cattle range. Sheep might get fat on it, but never cattle. Yet once you come on this side of it, onto the Concho Creek range, you're on good land again.

"If Tasker Gentry and I allowed one granger in on Concho Creek, in no time at all there'd be a flock of them. So we've set Concho Creek up as a dead line. Big Dan Sharples understands that, but he's constantly scheming to put grangers on the creek, and so get control of it. To which, Tasker Gentry and I say no! There you have the kernel of the nut."

Jim Larribee smoked silently for a little time, sucking his cigarette down to a stub which he let die, then crushed to pieces between thumb and forefinger. Abruptly he gave Fredericks the same kind of intent scrutiny that the cattleman had given him.

"That the whole core of trouble between you and Gentry and Sharples?"

"For Tasker Gentry, yes," said Fredericks. "For me, no. The other thing between Sharples and me is a personal thing. No matter what other reason Big Dan may give out publicly for wanting to get a foothold on Concho Creek, his real purpose is to break me, break and ruin me. And if I end up dead in the scuffle, so much the better."

"You make out a pretty rough case against the man," Larribee said quietly. "And there is generally another side to any argument."

"Yes," conceded Fredericks, "generally there is. But not in this one. Judge for yourself. After leaving your office last night I stopped at the Acme Mercantile. I made a final try at talking sense to Sharples. I suggested we call it quits—that we live and let live. Do you know the answer I got?"

John Fredericks leaned forward in his chair, his words running harsh.

"He called me mealy mouthed and accused me of being afraid of the high cards he held, whatever the hell he thinks they are. He wound up telling me to get off his property. So I make no more tries at talking peace with that fellow. I'll stay in my end of this valley, but by God, he and his grangers better stay in their end. Because, if Sharples ever forces this thing to a shoot-out, I waste no time or effort on his collection of two-legged dogs. I go after *him*—personally! If killing is what he must have, then he'll get it. I'll end his business for him, once and for all. I told him as much, and he damn' well better believe I meant it!"

Stirred with his uprush of feeling, Fredericks got to his feet and took a short turn along the porch. Jim Larribee stood, ready to leave. Then Kelsey Fredericks stepped out the door. She had donned a little frilled apron over her dress and she carried a tray with two steaming cups on it. She stopped near Larribee.

"Dad always likes another cup of coffee at this time of the morning. You'll join him?"

Larribee tipped his head. "This is good of you."

He held her glance closely as he spoke, and for one great, intense moment his true feeling for her lay clear for her to see. Here was the message that for him she was a dawn wind, sweeping down pure and cool off the clean-scented slopes of the Sabines: here the word that she was the whole breadth and depth of the best day of his life. These things his glance told her as surely as if he'd shouted them aloud.

She caught her breath, her eyes widening, while color flooded the soft hollow of her throat and ran truant through her cheeks. She turned quickly away and carried coffee to her father. Then she went on along the porch to fuss for a moment with the hammock, brushing it out, adjusting some pillows.

When she came back to reclaim the two empty coffee cups, her glance and manner were impersonal and unrevealing. She accepted Larribee's murmured thanks with a matter-of-fact nod and turned into the house.

John Fredericks stood beside Larribee at the edge of the porch. "If it's agreeable with you, I'll keep a man permanently on Concho Creek and have Tasker Gentry do the same. And in the future, head off any of Big Dan Sharples' crowd before they have time to light."

"No!" Jim Larribee turned on the cattleman quickly. "Nobody puts men on Concho Creek. If that creek is a dead line from one direction, it is from the other. So long as it remains the center of trouble, neither side stays on it. I'll see to that."

Color flared briefly in Fredericks' face at the abrupt bluntness of this retort and ultimatum. Then, as the fairness of it came to him, he nodded.

"Let it stand so." Further thought came to him. "You say you stopped by the Gentry place, talked with Old Tasker. You see anything of Fitch?"

Larribee shook his head.

"The old man was pretty bitter about Fitch breaking his word and pulling that runout. I asked him where Fitch was and he said flatly that he didn't know. I believe him. So now," wryly, "all I got to do to find Fitch is ride a thousand miles of territory, more or less, and trust to luck."

That morning, Dobe Lear had ridden out of Silver Ford during the black, very early hours, long before the town came awake. He headed upvalley and reached Concho Creek while the stars were still high and bright. Part of the errand that was taking him on this ride was to see Curly Gibson and tell him that Big Dan Sharples wanted him in town. But that was a secondary thing, and he could see Curly on his way back. So Dobe did not rouse the sleeping cabin.

He went on, angling northwest toward the Maacama Rim until even with the Gentry headquarters. There he stopped, and from a fair distance watched daylight break across the Sabines and the ranch yonder stir and quicken to life.

Dobe carried Big Dan Sharples' order to get in touch with Boardy Samuels and deliver to him a message. By necessity, this must be done secretly, which posed a problem that framed a troubled scowl on Dobe's narrow face, while he smoked a match-thin cigarette and waited and watched.

He heard the distant clangor of the cook-shack gong, saw the crew cross from bunkhouse to cook shack. After breakfast they caught and saddled and headed toward the rim. Dobe found hiding for his horse and himself in a thin scatter of brush that edged out from the rim, and he watched the riders file by at a jog some hundred yards distant. Boardy Samuels was one of them. With them they led four pack horses, loaded with gear. Plainly these men would not be returning to headquarters for a few days at least. When they disappeared into the rough country below the rim, Dobe set about following cautiously.

It was around midafternoon when Boardy Samuels, riding alone for the first time that day, began working out a series of brushy pockets tucked away under a remote stringer of Maacama Rim. Now and then he flushed a head or two of cattle into the open. Boardy brought no great interest to his work and a scowling discontent lay on his broad, swart face.

Boardy Samuels had never been able to forget the days when he rode as sheriff up and down the Pride River Valley. Those had been the best days of his life. The pay was fine, the work relatively easy. Sitting in a sheriff's saddle put a man up there, lifted him above the ordinary run. Carrying the star, a man drew plenty of water, threw a lot of shadow. Authority lived with him. When he rode down the trail, other men reined aside.

But working cattle was working cattle, even if a man did ride as foreman and could make other men move to his order. It could mean long, long hours—daylight-to-dark hours. It could, on occasion, mean what lay ahead now for the next few days, a rough camp back in rough country, hunkering on your heels to eat and sleeping on the ground. A damn' Siwash sort of existence, Boardy told himself sourly.

But when a man was sheriff he took his meals in town at the Riverside Hotel or the White Stag eating house. He could drop in at the Maverick Bar for a drink or two, any time the notion hit. And at night he slept on a good bed under a roof.

Boardy thrashed through the dragging, stubborn brush of another pocket, found it empty of any cattle, and emerged to find Dobe Lear looking at him past his horse's ears. Boardy set back abruptly, bleak and darkly wary.

"What the hell are you doing here?"

"Looking for you," Dobe answered. "Big Dan sent me with a message."

"Big Dan! What message would he be sending me?"

"He wants to see you, soon as possible."

Boardy's thoughts circled warily about this word. He searched for a reason Big Dan Sharples would have for wanting to see him, and could think of none. There was a lot more to this thing that he had to know about. He brought smoking out of a shirt pocket and began building a cigarette.

"It don't make sense, Lear. I've never been on Big Dan's side of the fence or him on mine. He spent a lot of time and effort and money taking my sheriff's star away from me and pinning it on that fellow Larribee. So I can't figure a single good reason why he'd want to see me about anything."

Dobe shrugged.

"All I know is what he told me to do. He told me to locate you and tell you to come see him. He said to ask you how you'd like to be sheriff again. Now I've done it. The rest is up to you."

Boardy, a sputtering sulphur match cupped in his hands and halfway to the cigarette in his lips, went completely still and stayed just so while the match burned to a stub and singed his fingers. He cursed softly at the bite of pain and rubbed his finger tips on the leather of his saddle skirt while staring at Dobe with eyes sparked to a sudden glitter.

"Did I hear right? Big Dan said to ask how I'd like to be sheriff again?"

"That's it," Dobe said.

"It makes less sense than ever, now."

Dobe shrugged again. "I don't know nothin' about that, and I don't give a damn. I've found you and I've told you, which was all I was supposed to do. Now I'm heading back to town." He lifted his reins.

"A minute," said Boardy. "I got to think on this."

Here was a proposition that had to be looked at from both sides and these sides weighed, one against the other. In this thing somewhere, Boardy could sense a double cross, but for the life of him he couldn't see where Big Dan had the slightest thing to gain by double-crossing him. So that treatment was surely reserved for somebody else. And that somebody else had to be none other than Jim Larribee!

The glitter in Boardy Samuels' eyes deepened with the thought. Nothing in all the world would suit him more than to see that star stripped off Larribee and handed back to him. That would be something!

Boardy's pulse began to pound. The more he considered this thing the better it looked, the greater it appealed. The fact that if he did meet with Big Dan Sharples and arrange a deal with him meant turning his back on Tasker Gentry and John Fredericks—men who had stood by him in the past and done their best for him—bothered Boardy not at all.

Playing along with Fredericks and Gentry had got him nothing in the past, so he told himself now. Their backing hadn't been enough to keep him in office as sheriff, while Big Dan Sharples' opposition had been enough to throw him out. This, boiled down to hard facts, meant that, politically, Big Dan carried the weight in the valley. And the heavy side, the weighty side, was always the smart side to be on—in politics or out. . . .

Boardy scratched another match and this time lighted his cigarette. He looked through the smoke at Dobe Lear.

"Tell Big Dan I'll see him—tonight. May be a little late, but I'll be there!"

6

It was around half-past nine when Grant Hilliker, a final cigar fresh burning between his teeth, left the Maverick Bar and stood for a long moment at the street corner, savoring night's fine cool flavor. After which, he turned left down River Street and went along past Cap Porter's saddle shop, past Abe Chain's livery barn and corral, and so on to the river ford.

He often took this little walk at night before going to his room in the Riverside Hotel. It offered him the opportunity to get completely away from town and so know an interval of the full, rewarding peace a man might find only by seeking some spot of solitude.

Down here close to the river the only sounds were the good, natural sounds; the soft chuckle of running water, the stir and rustle of the small wild life that used the night to move about in. Occasionally the distant yammer of a coyote echoed in out of the far dark, or the pure, cool call of the nighthawk drifted down from heaven's star-pierced vastness: sounds that were not so much sounds as they were a part of the measured beat of Creation's pulse.

Where many men might have missed these sure, free rewards of sensory observation, Grant Hilliker had the perception to flavor them deeply and fully, and after a fine peaceful half hour with them, he would go back to his bed relaxed and comforted and thoroughly in balance again.

Lurking in the black maw of Abe Chain's stable door, Curly Gibson watched the slim, taut, quick-striding figure of the lawyer pass and presently slipped out to follow. Hulking and thick-set though he was, Curly could move softly when he chose, and so he moved now, a half crouched, stalking shadow in the dark.

Coming in closer to the river across a stretch of open, which offered no deeper shadows by building or corral to skulk in, Curly slowed his pace and so lost Hilliker in the dark. After a little, however, he located him again, first by a drift of cigar smoke, and then more exactly by the wink of the cigar's glowing tip, a point of sharp crimson against the blackness. Hilliker had moved downstream a little.

Curly circled cautiously, low and stealthy, to come in on Hilliker from behind, across a stretch of yielding, sound-muffling sand. The voice of the river, low muted though it was, helped silence Curly's approach. He covered the last few yards in a heavy, lunging rush, throwing a driving punch as he came. His fist smashed into the back of Hilliker's head, just where head and neck joined, and the slender lawyer, hit with the wickedest kind of rabbit punch, went over on his face as though he'd been shot.

Grant Hilliker was not completely knocked out but he was so close to it, so numbed all over, he was incapable of recognizing his assailant, of calling for help or putting up any resistance at all to what followed.

It was methodically, savagely brutal. If there was any touch of mercy in it anywhere, it lay in the fact that when Curly hauled Hilliker half upright and began smashing a fist into his face, the second of these blows drove all consciousness out of the lawyer, and he felt nothing of the balance.

Curly Gibson made the best of the opportunity. He'd had his orders. Grant Hilliker, so Big Dan had said, talked too much and needed a lesson. Give him one, he'd told Curly, and make it a good one. So Curly set out to follow orders to the letter.

When he finished, Curly's fists felt numb and his arms weary. And Grant Hilliker was a crumpled heap of battered, blood-spattered stillness on the sand. Curly left him so and went back to town.

Sometime later, little Abe Chain came out of his stable and hurried down to the river ford. He looked and he listened, but when he neither heard or saw sign of anyone around, he began to call, not too softly, not too loud.

"Mr. Hilliker! Mr. Hilliker!"

Getting no answer, Abe began to search,

his movements quickening until he was fairly running, up and down, here and there, pausing once or twice to call again.

"Mr. Hilliker—Mr. Hilliker—!"

He found Grant Hilliker by practically falling over him. Abe scratched a match, had his look, then began to whimper, tears running down his wrinkled cheeks. He was as curious, as garrulous as a jaybird, was Abe Chain, but he was also a gentle-hearted little man, with a great capacity for pity and for righteous courage. He showed both now.

He had almost to lie down in the sand beside Grant Hilliker to get the seemingly lifeless figure across his shoulder, but he managed it finally and then somehow found strength to push to his knees and from there to his feet, under the limp weight of a man who weighed more than he did himself.

After that, without a single pause, Abe Chain carried his burden back to the stable and laid it carefully down on his own bunk in the harness room. Then, painfully straightening, little Abe braced his back against the wall to keep from going down himself.

His heart was thunder in his chest, his breath a choking rasp in a throat thickened with a salty slime. He was dizzy with the nausea of exhaustion and for a time there was no anchor to his thoughts. Gradually, however, things grew more orderly, and with this physical quieting and steadying, coherence returned. Abe got a lantern going and had another look at Grant Hilliker, seeking certainty that the lawyer was still alive. He was.

The closest medic was Doc Shields, and a good one, Abe knew. But Doc Shields, who had once had office here in Silver Ford, now had it in the granger settlement at Ten Mile. As Doc explained the move, it was to be closer to the source of what had become ninety per cent of his business.

Granger families, Doc Shields said, meant babies being born and mothers to be cared for. Granger families meant children, kids of all ages and coming down with all sorts of kid ailments. Measles, mumps, chicken pox, croup: occasionally the grimmer ones, like diphtheria, when a man had to be handy and work fast.

Before deciding on his move to Ten Mile, Doc said he'd just about worn out a buckboard and himself, driving back and forth on emergency calls at all times of day and night. So now, Doc Shields was hours away, and little Abe Chain could think of only one other answer, which sent him out into the night again, hurrying.

Hannah Virgil, a widow of many years, was a straight, somewhat gaunt woman who had known more than her share of life's rugged phases without losing a ready sense of humor or the well of genuine compassion which lay inherent in all good women. She was preparing for bed when an anxious, persistent knocking at her door brought her to it, lamp in hand. In a full-length robe and with her white hair loose about her head, she made an almost stately figure. She looked down at Abe Chain in some surprise.

"Why, Abe—what on earth would you be wanting at this time of night? What's wrong?"

"It's Grant Hilliker, Hannah. I got him in my harness room. He's been hurt—bad. And—"

"Hurt, how?" broke in Hannah Virgil.

"Like somebody beat him," Abe said. "I thought you might come and look after him while I go down to Ten Mile after Doc Shields."

Hannah Virgil's glance had been steadily on little Abe's face as he explained. Now she nodded, and gently said:

"Of course, Abe. Just as soon as I make myself decent."

Shortly they were hurrying back to the stable together. Abe turned up the lantern and held it while Hannah Virgil made her examination of the man lying so still on the bunk. Hannah Virgil caught her breath, and a low, stern anger broke from her.

"Who did this to him? What two-legged animal is responsible?"

Abe's answer was a little indirect. "I found him lying down by the river. Mr. Hilliker often goes for a stroll down that way of nights. I saw him go by, but when he didn't come back and didn't come back, I got to worryin', and I went looking for him. I found him just like he is now, and brought him here."

"You carried him all the way up from the river by yourself?" Hannah Virgil marveled.

"Yes."

She dropped a hand on Abe's shoulder.

"Good man! Now, before you start after Doc Shields, go rouse Maria Rojas and send her here. Maria's a fine hand at anything of this sort. And"—here the stern anger burned in her tone again—"I hope the animal responsible for this comes prowling to finish the job. It would give me a chance to stick a pitchfork through him!"

Big Dan Sharples and Boardy Samuels sat in the kitchen behind the Acme Mercantile. Both had cigars in their lips, which Big Dan had supplied. Both had whisky in front of them, which Big Dan had also supplied. Big Dan had been talking, feeling his way cautiously. Now Boardy threw up a hand.

"No need of all this backing and filling, Sharples. You had Dobe Lear ask me if I'd like to be sheriff. I'm here, ain't I? You got a proposition, let's hear it."

"Good enough!" growled Big Dan. "I like straight talk, myself. Here it is. I'm not satisfied the way Larribee is handling his job. He's gone stubborn on me and is full of a lot of damn' fool ideas. So, out he goes. In his place I want a man who will play along with me—all the way! Still interested?"

Boardy considered warily. "Why pick me? Time was when you'd liked to cut my throat."

Big Dan nodded. "Right! But it wasn't personal. Then you were the other side. On my side, you and me'll get along fine."

Boardy drew deep on his cigar. "You say Larribee is done. How you goin' to get rid of him?"

"Simple enough," Big Dan said. "For what they judge sufficient cause, the county commissioners can at any time take the star off a sheriff. I'm a county commissioner. Ira Redstone and Bert Carter are the other two. They do what I tell them to do. There you have it. We fire one sheriff, we appoint a new one. Could be you."

Boardy smoked over this one, too, before putting his narrowed glance on Big Dan.

"If the county commissioners can do all you say, how was it you didn't fire me when I was packing the star and working with Fredericks and Gentry?"

"I wasn't sure enough of my strength, then," admitted Big Dan candidly. "I had to wait for the election that put Larribee in and you out. After that, I knew where and how strong I stood, and what I could do."

Boardy nodded to the logic of the explanation, then asked:

"What cause you going to call against Larribee? You can't just say: 'All right, Larribee, you're done. We don't like the way you slice your meat.' You got to offer more than that, or the grangers down at Ten Mile and the little hill ranchers could start wondering and asking hard-to-answer questions. Those people voted for Larribee; he's their sheriff. Maybe they won't like him kicked out without a thank you or what the hell."

Big Dan leaned back in his chair. "A good question. Shows you're thinking. But you're forgetting something too: a man named Price Tedrow, a granger who was mighty popular down around Ten Mile. He got in an argument with Fitch Gentry and Fitch killed him. Oh, it might very well have been what Fitch claimed—an even break. The slug Fitch got through the leg certainly points that way. But that's neither here nor there. Down at Ten Mile the grangers say it was murder, and they want Fitch's scalp.

"Well, where is Fitch now? On the loose, after being safely in custody. Whose fault? Larribee's. Fitch made a fool of him. Talked up right, that fact gets bigger and bigger. So, when the board of county commissioners fires Larribee for being incompetent, do you think much objection will show around Ten Mile? I don't."

Boardy squinted at the ceiling through the smoke of his cigar. Then he looked at Big Dan again.

"You figger things pretty fine, for a fact. But I ask you this. Suppose Larribee refuses to hand over the star? Suppose he tells the board of county commissioners to go to hell and stands ready to make an open fight of it?"

"He hasn't a chance," Big Dan said. "Any man in political office stays there only so long as he can muster the necessary support. And what could Larribee count on, once we turn our backs on him?"

"How about John Fredericks and Tasker Gentry?" Boardy asked. "There's no middle ground in this valley. It's one side or the other. You go against a man, then Fredericks and Gentry are almost sure to back him."

"Their backing wasn't strong enough to keep you in office," Big Dan pointed out.

"No," admitted Boardy, "it wasn't. But that's no sign you can write them off like they were a pair of sheepherders. Should the idea ever hit them to quit fighting you politically, and instead buckle on their guns, then you'd better have some damn' good answers ready."

Big Dan rolled his cigar back and forth in his heavy lips the way he always did when gripped with impatience.

"I'm wondering if you really want to wear the

star again, Samuels. All you've done so far is bring up doubts of this and that."

Boardy's swarthy face hardened and he traded measuring stare for measuring stare.

"You said you liked plain talk, Sharples. Let's have some. The double cross is running all through this deal. You're double-crossing Larribee; I'm double-crossing Tasker Gentry and John Fredericks. Which is quite all right with me—I'm no way squeamish, so long as I get what I want. But I don't blunder around blind. So I ask questions. Here's another one. Why did you send for *me* in particular?"

Big Dan backed deftly away from the mood he'd roused in Boardy. His words and tone turned bland.

"Because I knew you and me were two of a kind. We both know what we want and we go after it, no matter how we have to play to get it. You got any idea where Fitch Gentry is?"

Startled, Boardy's glance flared a trifle. "Maybe he's out at the ranch."

Big Dan shook his head. "You know he wouldn't be."

"Why wouldn't he?"

"Plain common sense. He's on the dodge, with Larribee looking for him. First place Larribee would check on is the ranch."

A glint of suspicion showed in Boardy's eyes. Plainly he was asking himself if this was another double cross of some kind. Big Dan shrewdly guessed Boardy's thought and went on with a quick blandness.

"You said when I pulled my support away from Larribee, he might find some in Tasker Gentry and John Fredericks. I've something in mind to head off any chance of that. To make it work, I'd have to locate Fitch."

Boardy considered, still scowling. Then, grudgingly: "Say I do know where Fitch is. What's your angle?"

Big Dan gave out with it slowly, feeling his way with every word.

"Larribee's looking for Fitch, and with his nose way out of joint because Fitch made him look so damn' silly by that getaway. It's reasonable, don't you think, that people would generally feel that Larribee is out to get even, no matter how rough he has to be?"

"Maybe," admitted Boardy. "But I still don't get what you're driving at."

Big Dan mouthed his cigar reflectively. "Suppose Fitch were found dead—wherever he is? You think Tasker Gentry would put his support behind the man he figured had killed Fitch?"

Boardy stared. "Should Larribee happen to locate Fitch, he'll put handcuffs on him again, not kill him. Not unless Fitch insists on trying to shoot it out. Which he won't. Strictly on his own, there ain't much salt in Fitch."

"Larribee doesn't have to kill him," Big Dan said smoothly. "Just so it *appears* he's the one who did."

Now at last Boardy began to get it, and the implications held him still. He met Big Dan's hooded glance for a long moment before speaking slowly.

"Damned if you're not the coldest proposition I ever met up with, Sharples."

Big Dan shrugged. "If you sit into a game at all, you sit in it to win. And at times, to do that, you got to turn rough. Say I am a cold proposition, Boardy, how cold are you? How bad do you want that star again?"

Big Dan poured fresh drinks while he spoke. His moves, his words were almost casual but inside he was tight drawn and alert. For here was the point where he got hold of Boardy completely, or had Boardy shy off just as completely.

Boardy sat leaning forward, elbows on the table, shoulders hunched so his head was drawn deep down between them. Tautness stiffened his broad, dark cheeks, and his eyes were heavy with a narrowed brooding.

He was recalling the days when he had ridden behind the star: when he was up there in the center of the trail, with other men reining aside to let him pass. When he was Sheriff Samuels, not just Boardy—cowhand . . .

He gulped the drink Big Dan had poured for

him and pushed his glass out for another refill.

"It's a deal," he growled. "I want that star again—bad enough!"

Big Dan got rid of a deep sigh of hidden, inner relief. He lifted his glass. "Let's drink on that."

Boardy put down his emptied glass, wiped his lips. "One more question, Dan. You say the grangers at Ten Mile want to see Fitch's scalp. The word gets around that Larribee's collected it, won't they be for Larribee?"

"To a degree, perhaps," Big Dan said drily. "But by that time Larribee will be an ex-sheriff. Where is Fitch?"

"Holed up in one of the old drifts of the North Star Basin Mine. I'm to take some grub to him first of next week."

"Does old Tasker know where he is?"

"Nobody knows where Fitch is but him and me—and you, now."

"Fine," Big Dan nodded. "The first of next week is the perfect time for Fitch Gentry to be found dead."

Again Boardy's muddy eyes met Big Dan's hooded ones. He nodded.

"When you goin' to move against Larribee?"

"The board of county commissioners will meet officially tomorrow morning. Out front, in my store. So nobody can claim it was something cooked up behind closed doors, I'm inviting

Tom Ivy to be present." A cynical, sardonic twist touched briefly at Big Dan's heavy lips.

"And we'll get together again, before long?" Boardy said.

"Before long," Big Dan nodded. "We'll give the citizens a chance to digest the word that they've lost one sheriff before we hand them the name of the new one—which will be—Boardy Samuels. Another drink for the trail?"

On riding away from the Fredericks ranch, Jim Larribee made a long, full day of it, first heading well up into the Sabines and ferreting through them before crossing the valley again at its far northern end and working south under the afternoon shadow of the Maacama Rim. Along the way he crossed a number of lonely trails and studied each for fresh sign, without success, and had a look at several old line-camp cabins he knew about.

His hope, of course, was to pick up some trace of Fitch Gentry, but he found nothing. He even rode far enough to take a look at the old Bentlow pack trail, and from there cut over to the Soldier Creek Road and looked this over carefully, nowhere finding what he wanted. Nor did he meet with or see anyone until, late in the afternoon, while working down through the Pot Holes country under the Maacama Rim, he came across a couple of Gentry saddle hands, shagging cattle out of the roughs and brushy gulches. He questioned them, but they claimed—apparently in all truth—to know nothing of where Fitch was.

With sundown at hand, he came in on Concho Creek again, and of a sudden knew an impulse to spend the night here in old and well-remembered surroundings. On leaving town early that morning, and unsure when he'd get back, he had tied a meager grub pack behind his saddle cantle, so with his food problem solved for the night, he reined up along the creek toward the cabin. And there met Kelsey Fredericks, sitting her saddle quietly, watching him approach.

To cover up the warm gust of feeling Larribee knew at sight of her, he turned particularly gruff, touching his hat, then saying flatly, "You shouldn't be here."

Her chin lifted. "And why not?"

"I ran a couple of unsavory characters off the creek this morning. They might have come back."

"And I should be concerned about that?"

"You should. For some reasons that make sense to me and more that don't, this creek is a battleground between your father and Big Dan Sharples. The feeling on both sides is piling up. As Kelsey Fredericks, that feeling could touch you, unpleasantly."

"Since I was old enough to ride alone, I've been coming here," she argued. "The falls—the pool—always they've been a favorite retreat of mine. The first time I ever saw you was a day when I rode in to this very spot and found you building that cabin."

"Just so," nodded Larribee. Then, drily, he added, "And lit out for home to spread the word. Which, in time, led to me being kicked out."

She colored. "You'd have been found out, anyway."

"Of course. And I'm not holding it against you, understand. But we're getting away from the main point. Which is, while the pulling and hauling goes on over this creek range, you shouldn't ride it alone."

Again her chin tilted. "No one would dare touch me."

"There was a drunk at Soldier Creek who tried to put a hand on you."

Again she colored, looking at him across the deepening shadows of sundown, a veiled inscrutability in her glance.

"You persist in showing concern over the welfare of John Fredericks' daughter, don't you? I can't help but wonder why, and how much of the concern is real."

"I never waste time being unreal about anything that counts," Larribee said. "And you could count more than you dream. Now, I think you'd better dust it for home."

Still looking at him in that veiled way, she lifted her reins.

"Yes," she said, a trifle breathlessly. "Yes, I think I'd better."

Her horse, a trim, fast-jogging dun, soon carried her out of sight along the downstream trail. Larribee pulled in beside the cabin and stepped from his saddle. In the very last of evening's light he cared for his horse, then cooked and ate a frugal supper. After which, cigarette smoke curling about his head, he sauntered up beside the pool that caught the plunging vigor of the falls and stood there in the clotted, velvet dark.

The voice of the falling water was a steady, liquid crashing, muted and subdued by the patient weight of night's wide silences. A churning mist whipped up and came as a fresh, cool breath. Here a man could relax fully and let his cares slip away from him, and, for a little time at least, stand well apart from the embroilments and cross purposes of other men.

It was a good hour before he returned to the cabin and spread his blanket on the bunk.

Up in the dim newness of the dawn, he cooked a pot of coffee and then was on his way to town, riding in at Abe Chain's livery barn just before the sun cracked its first ray across the Sabines. In front of the stable was a team and buckboard he'd seen many times, rolling here and there about the valley on errands of mercy and help. What, he wondered, would Doc Shields be doing here in Silver Ford this early in the morning?

As Larribee dismounted, it was Rita Rojas who came hurrying from the stable door. Her piquant young face was very sober, her eyes big and dark. She carried a pail in either hand and, at sight of Larribee, exclaimed with relief:

"Jeem! It is good you are here. Mister Hilliker, he is hurt. My mama, she is in there, helping. I go for hot water."

She would have darted off, but Larribee barred the way with an outthrust arm. His voice rang harshly.

"Grant Hilliker—hurt! How?"

"I do not know for sure. W'at I do know, it makes Doctor Shields swear w'ile he works. I must hurry—!"

She scurried away, brown feet twinkling. Larribee moved into the long, shadowy gallery of the stable, cold from night's lingering chill, acridly odorous from the stalls out back. There was another odor, a medicinal one—that of iodoform, biting, penetrating. It came from the harness room, where sounded the muted growl of Doc Shields' voice.

Abe Chain was hunched against an oat bin. He straightened up and looked at Larribee.

"Jim, something should sure be done about this." Larribee, his stomach muscles tightening, moved into the harness room. Hannah Virgil stood at the head of the wall bunk, Maria Rojas at the foot of it, both holding lanterns which fought back a slowly departing gloom. Doc Shields was down on one knee, sleeves rolled up, white hair bristling, a growling wrath in his throat as he worked over the figure lying on the bunk. At the sound of Larribee's careful step and the soft tinkle of a dragging spur rowel, Doc swore irritably.

"Goddamn it! I told Abe not to let in every curious Tom, Dick and—"

"Easy, Doc," cut in Larribee quietly. "I got a right to be curious."

Doc glanced up, squinting through steel-rimmed spectacles. His growl mellowed.

"Oh, it's you. Well, have your look."

Larribee had it, past Doc's shoulder, and at sight of Grant Hilliker's face, the tightening of his belly muscles became a solid knot.

"How bad, Doc?" His voice was thin and dry.

"Casually observed, you don't see the worst," Doc said. "Clinically speaking, we've got to deal with a degree of concussion, bruises and cuts and a couple of loosened teeth. These we can handle. Given time and a little treatment, these things will heal and clear up. But there's an angle apart from the physical that could be dangerous."

"What do you mean?" Larribee asked.

"Like this," Doc said. "Grant Hilliker was a sensitive, idealistic man. With such, a beating like this can leave a mental and spiritual bruise that never does thoroughly heal."

"Who did it, Doc?"

"I don't know. I wish I did. Yes, by God—I wish I did! Hannah, bring that lantern just a little closer. That's it. Steady, right there!"

And Doc was at his work again, entirely engrossed.

Jim Larribee went quietly out. There was nothing he could do here that would help. In him a bright, cold rage had begun to flame, deepening with every breath. He caught Abe Chain by the arm and drew him along to the stable entrance and faced him there as the sun's first rays began to run the length of River Street.

"All right, Abe. Maybe you know something about it?"

Abe nodded. "Maybe."

"You see it done?"

"No." Little Abe, up all night, rubbed a hand tiredly across his face. "Maybe you better let me tell it my own way, Jim."

"Just so you tell!"

"Well," said Abe, "you know how Mr. Hilliker nearly always takes a walk down by the river at night? I've seen him go by here so many times. . . . Last night I was over at Cap Porter's for a couple of games of cribbage. Just when I was leavin', I saw Mr. Hilliker go by, as usual.

"I had a sick bronc out in my back corral I

wanted to take a look at before goin' to bed. Which I did, and when I came into the stable by the back way, I see this feller duck out into the street through this door."

"What fellow?" demanded Larribee.

Abe hesitated, then shrugged.

"It was pretty dark, but I had him outlined against the starlight in the street. You know how Curly Gibson's shoulders hunch up so it looks like he ain't got any neck? Well, that's the way this feller looked."

"What did he do after he ducked out?"

"Headed down toward the river. I kept wondering about him, and then, when Mr. Hilliker didn't come back from the river, I got a queer feeling about things. So I went down there myself. I didn't see no more of Curly Gibson, but I found Mr. Hilliker layin' on the sand like you just saw him. I managed to get him over my shoulder and packed him in. Then I got Hannah Virgil to look after him while I rode down to Ten Mile after Doc Shields. That's it, Jim. That's all of it, far as I know."

"Thanks, Abe," said Larribee tightly. "Thanks!"

He moved out into the street and along it. He saw Bert Carter emerge from the Riverside Hotel and stand waiting for Ira Redstone, who came up Valley Street from his stage station and freight yards. After which, the pair angled across to the Acme Mercantile porch, where Big Dan Sharples stood high and ponderously angular in the flare of the early sun.

At the corner, Larribee met Tom Ivy, just leaving the Maverick Bar. A broad and stocky man, the saloon owner was tough enough to act the bouncer in his own establishment when occasion required, yet was a square and likeable man. He paused as Larribee, jerking a nod toward the bar door, asked:

"Any early customers in there, Tom?"

"Nobody there but Johnny Pike, swamping out," Ivy said. "Who you lookin' for?"

"Curly Gibson."

"Ain't seen him since last night. He was in then, pretty late. He broke a glass on me."

"Broke a glass?"

"Dropped it when he went to lift his drink off the bar. His right hand was jammed up some, swollen and with the knuckles skinned. He said he'd hurt it, ropin' down a bronc. What you want him for, Jim?"

Larribee, twisting up a smoke, did not answer right away and, in the pause, Big Dan Sharples' voice came carrying.

"All right, Tom! We got business to take care of."

Larribee, a match glowing in his cupped hands, lighted his cigarette and peered through the smoke.

"What's all the hurry so early in the morning?

Business must be pretty damned important."

Tom Ivy shrugged. "A meeting of the county commissioners, so Dobe Lear said last night. For some reason, Big Dan wants me to sit in on it. Past that, I don't know a thing."

Larribee took two deep drags at his cigarette before flipping the butt into the street's dust with a gesture of curt decision.

"I'll walk over with you, Tom. I want a word with Big Dan Sharples."

7

By the time Jim Larribee and Tom Ivy crossed the street and climbed the steps of the Acme Mercantile, Big Dan Sharples had retreated behind a barrier of wariness, his hooded eyes reflecting a hard and speculative glint. He put his glance on Larribee and tried to keep his voice bland.

"Something you wanted?"

Meeting the glance, Jim Larribee found himself suddenly despising this man, coldly and thoroughly, while knowing a small moment of silent marveling at how this change of sentiment could come so abruptly and how Sharples, physically, now stood so sinister in his eyes. He had always seen Big Dan as an ugly man, but with the judgment of a friendship which accepted and approved, regardless. Now, with that unconscious generosity stripped aside, what he saw struck him as evil and forbidding. His answer was curt.

"Yes—something. Where's Curly Gibson?"

The flat hostility in Larribee's voice made Big Dan slow to answer. He covered the interval by selecting a cigar from a vest pocket, gnawing off the tip of it and getting it alight. When he finally spoke, his glance was fixed four inches below Larribee's chin.

"I don't know where he is. What do you want him for?"

"You know damn' well what I want him for!"

A mottled flush ran through Big Dan's heavy cheeks. "Don't use that tone of voice with me. I won't stand for it."

"You'll stand for it and like it. Where's Gibson? Come on—speak up!"

Bert Carter coughed uneasily. Ira Redstone made a restless half turn that took him a yard or two farther away, porch boards creaking under his step. Tom Ivy made no sound or move, save the quick flicker of his glance, which touched Larribee, then Big Dan, then returned to Larribee. In Big Dan's cheeks the mottled flush deepened angrily.

"So you want me to speak up, eh? Very well. I doubt you'll care for what you hear. As a sheriff, Larribee, the county commissioners have decided you're incompetent. The latest proof is the way you've blundered the Fitch Gentry job. So we're taking the star off you!"

Very still for a long moment, Larribee regarded Big Dan narrowly. Here was something that had not, until this moment, entered his mind. The possibility that something of this sort might come up . . . He had wondered many times if the voters would give him a second term in office, or if, through some twist of reasoning, turn against him and elect someone else. Any elective office was politics, and political favor ever a chancy thing. But this—!

Here was the heavy, ruthless hand of Big Dan Sharples at work again, beating ponderously and without mercy toward some dark objective. Big Dan, using men to his own ends so long as they answered strictly to his will and order, but tossing them callously aside the moment they dared defy him and stand straight and unafraid in their own right.

The inner fire that had sent Jim Larribee looking for Curly Gibson flared ever hotter.

"This," he said, thinly caustic, "has all the earmarks of a fine and fancy double cross. You in on it, Tom?"

"No!" The saloon owner rapped out the word with convincing emphasis. "Not me, Jim. Sharples, to hell with you and your meeting!"

Larribee laughed, little mirth in the sound.

"That's the way to talk. I say the same. Sharples, you're getting way out ahead of yourself. The people voted this star on me. It stays there until they vote it off!"

He looked at Carter and Redstone, scorching them with his contempt.

"How long since you two straightened up to walk like men? You ought to try it again some time. Good for your shriveled souls. And you'd find the air a lot better, higher up!"

He turned back to Big Dan again. How right

Grant Hilliker had been in his outspoken estimate of this man! And because he had seen so clearly and spoken so honestly, he now lay senseless in Abe Chain's harness room, savagely misused and beaten. The gray rage in Jim Larribee surged higher.

"You ordered it done, didn't you, Sharples? You gave that damned animal, Curly Gibson, his orders. I'm sure of it. So, if Grant Hilliker's condition should turn for the worse, then . . ."

"What's this? What's this?" cut in Tom Ivy. "Jim, what about Grant Hilliker? What's wrong with him?"

"He's over in Abe Chain's harness room, all beat to hell. Doc Shields is working on him. You said Curly Gibson claimed he'd hurt his hand roping a bronc. He lied, Tom. They always lie, does Mister Big Dan Sharples and his crowd of trained dogs. The truth isn't in a single damn' one of them. Curly Gibson hurt his hand hitting Grant Hilliker with it. And who gives Curly his orders? Why, who do you think, Tom, if you just had one guess?"

Tom Ivy, looking at Big Dan, glimpsed the betraying flicker far back in those hooded eyes, and he spoke with deepening anger.

"Grant Hilliker is my good friend—a fine, intelligent gentleman. I've always felt it my privilege to know him. Jim, why was he beaten?"

"Because he saw this fellow Sharples as he

really is, and wasn't afraid to say so." Larribee drove his insistence at Big Dan again. "For the last time—where's Curly Gibson?"

A small thread of hidden panic was running now through Big Dan Sharples; he had been backed into a corner he hadn't foreseen. He could think of no answer for Larribee save denial, and he voiced it mechanically.

"I don't know where he is."

At that precise moment Dobe Lear stepped from the store door, speaking as he came.

"Any arnica around, Boss? Curly, he—"

Glimpsing Jim Larribee, Dobe went abruptly still.

Larribee murmured sardonically. "So! Arnica for Curly, eh? We'll see!"

He moved to the store door, putting a final scathing glance on Big Dan.

"Always the big lie, eh Dan? Always the big lie!"

On the broad of Jim Larribee's passing shoulders, Dobe Lear laid a look so charged with malevolence that Tom Ivy, observing, reacted with curt roughness. He swept a hard and expert forearm against Dobe, whirling him aside.

"This," said Tom Ivy, "I want to see. Dobe, keep out of it. You crowd in and I'll twist your damn' neck!"

Out back, in the kitchen of Big Dan's living quarters, Curly Gibson sat hunched in a chair.

Between his feet was a bucket of steaming water, and into this his right hand was dipped, forearm deep. When Curly had hit Grant Hilliker that first driving, treacherous blow to the back of the head, a sharp, breaking pain had shot through his fist. But lost in the viciousness of what followed, he had used the fist again and again on his victim, for the moment impervious to his own physical discomfort.

Hours ago, however, that brutal fire had burned out, and Curly's concern over the hand had kept pace with the steadily growing misery in it. It had grown swollen and clumsy, and there had been little sleep for its owner throughout the balance of the night. In consequence, Curly now felt parched and seedy and was in an evil humor. When the kitchen door opened, he figured it was Dobe Lear coming back.

"Locate any?" he growled, without looking up.

"No arnica, Curly!" And it wasn't Dobe Lear who answered.

Curly Gibson jerked straight in his chair, and for one long, frozen moment stared, reading beyond any mistake the bleak purpose in Jim Larribee's eyes. And what he saw there brought him lunging to his feet, the violence of the move upsetting the bucket of water. For greater freedom while doctoring his hand, Curly had stacked his belt and gun on the table. Now he made a dive for the weapon.

Jim Larribee caught up a chair and swung it.

"For Grant Hilliker!" he said.

The chair crashed down across Curly's head and shoulders, several rungs and one leg crumpling. The impact put Curly down. For a little time he lay dazed, a trickle of crimson showing in the thick mat of his hair, where that crumpled chair leg had split his scalp.

But this fellow was burly as a bear, and full of the same tenacity and brute resistance. He came rearing up in a savage, berserk rush.

Larribee swung the chair again.

Curly's move in throwing up a defending arm and hand was an instinctive one. But it was the injured hand, and when the chair smashed into it, a rioting bawl of agony erupted from Curly's lips. He stumbled back, hugging the battered hand in his left armpit, and tried to keep beyond Larribee's reach.

But the room was too small for that and Larribee, cornering his man against a wall, swung a third flailing blow which stripped the remaining three legs from the chair. By dodging desperately, Curly managed to take the worst of the impact on a hunched shoulder, and so kept his feet.

Realizing now that he had no chance in this affair unless he either got hold of his gun or laid hands on Larribee, Curly drove ahead once more and ran into the jabbing edge of the chair seat, which, catching him across the mouth and mashing his lips, sent him reeling back, sick and bleeding.

Remorselessly, Larribee moved in, set for another smash. Desperate, Curly charged, blindly reaching and grabbing. Larribee side-stepped and swung, coming up on his toes so as to get plenty behind the blow. The heavy edge of the chair caught Curly on the side of the head, just above the ear, and he crumpled limply under this one, never moving after piling up on the floor. Larribee prowled around him, chair half lifted.

From the kitchen doorway, shaken by the ruthlessness Larribee had shown him, Tom Ivy exclaimed:

"Not again, Jim—not again! You hit him again, you'll kill him!"

Larribee, silent for a moment, harshly said:

"Maybe. But it would be no loss!"

He threw the smashed-up chair aside and dragged a hand across his eyes, as though to wipe away some sort of feral haze. He tramped past Tom Ivy and through the store to the porch, where a silent, hostile group still stood. Here he paused, his challenging, bitter glance on Big Dan Sharples.

"He's in there on the floor. Should he ever lay hands on any friend of mine again, I'll really finish him. The rest of you—stay away from me. You hear? Stay away from me!"

He dropped down the steps, angled across and turned along River Street toward Abe Chain's stable.

Tom Ivy, who had followed Larribee out, paused at the top of the steps and had his say.

"This morning, Dan, you were set to use me for your own dirty purpose; to make a piece of slippery conniving, in which I had no part, look respectable. A man tries that sort of thing on me just once—and you've used up your turn. Jim Larribee said it, for both of us. Stay away from me!"

Expecting no answer, and getting none, Tom Ivy crossed to his Maverick Bar.

Bert Carter, ever the weakest of props, began dry-washing his hands nervously, his glance on Big Dan, waiting his word and will. Ira Redstone was also watching, something not far from mockery in his eyes.

Expecting an explosion of anger, they were surprised when none showed, at least not openly. The cords of Big Dan's throat were taut and swollen, there was congestion behind his eyes and his voice thick when he spoke. Yet his words fell almost softly.

"Dobe, go see about Curly." To Carter and Redstone: "You can get on with your own business. We'll have another talk, later."

Dobe and Redstone moved off, but Carter, uncertain and uneasy, lingered a moment.

"Where do we stand now, Dan? We tell Larribee he's through, and he defies us."

"He'll be told again—and it will stick!"

Alone, Big Dan appeared to be casually surveying the street. In reality, he was seeing none of it, for the fury he'd suppressed in front of the others was now wild in him, blinding him to all but his own seething thoughts. It was the lie that punished him; perhaps not so much the actual fabric of the lie as allowing himself to be caught in it.

Yeah—caught in it, with Larribee spilling contempt all over him, while others listened and looked on . . . !

Abruptly the morning sun seemed to hold a searching glare of hostility, and he craved shadow and seclusion in which to hide until he'd regained some measure of his old self-assurance. So he wheeled into the store, where old Charley Clark went his methodical way of caring for the simple mechanics of trade. In a far corner was the small cubby where the books of the establishment were kept and worked on, and here Big Dan Sharples sought a chair and settled back in brooding speculation.

As the immediate turmoil in him cooled somewhat, he made himself face up to the facts realistically. He had blundered, definitely and badly. It would do no good to blame Curly Gibson for not handling his chore more shrewdly; the fault was his own for setting Curly after Grant Hilliker at this time. That could have waited for the doing.

It was the old black anger that had betrayed him, the anger that was one of his greatest weaknesses, but also one of the real driving forces of his life; for it was the anger that fed the hate that spurred him ever relentlessly on in his reach for power.

This was one of the times it had misled him. He had tried to hit back at Jim Larribee too quickly, at the wrong time and place. And while the county commissioners did have the right to remove Larribee from office, with him defying them it could mean considerable time and legal process might be required.

Big Dan broke out a cigar, and over it brooded darkly. He should have waited until the deal he'd made with Boardy Samuels had born fruit; until Fitch was dead and the blame laid on Larribee, so that old Tasker Gentry would be on Larribee's trail too. One thing was very sure; the county commissioners could not afford to back away now. They had to go ahead, keeping the pressure on Larribee until he wilted.

Big Dan gnawed his cigar savagely as he thought of how carefully he had selected and groomed Jim Larribee to serve him as a useful pawn. Now Larribee was an obstacle instead of an aid in the way of the final objective.

The final objective!

Product of the distant years, growth of the evil seed of envy and jealousy planted far back in the days when Dan Sharples and John Fredericks were young, in a young country, with all the world theirs for the taking, when any challenge was to be reached for eagerly and the trails were wide and ran without limit.

They had known friendship in those distant days, he and John Fredericks, a friendship which held for a time even after Lutie Hammond brought her bright loveliness into their lives. But as the inevitable division set in, it had become more and more Lutie Hammond and John Fredericks, with Dan Sharples ever apart and farther away.

Oh, she had been kind toward him, Lutie had. Though it might have been pity, a thought which always made Big Dan writhe. But in the end it was John Fredericks whom she loved and married. And the day that marriage took place, Big Dan Sharples' life came all apart.

He had sought refuge in the bottle, and had gone far down into the blind and numbing depths of it. There, for a time and of a kind, he did find some semblance of oblivion. He found something else too. Hate. For John Fredericks.

It was old, now, that hate was; as old as the years reaching back to its beginning. Nor had it ever lessened. Instead, it had become an obsessive thing, a single dark, feral purpose in a man's life. It was a disease, a malignancy beyond all reason or conscience which had scarred its possessor past any chance of healing.

The goal of it was the destruction of John Fredericks. His certain death, finally. But not until he'd been beaten down and broken and ruined in every concrete way. John Fredericks must suffer all these things and know who brought them about.

Such was the venom of Big Dan Sharples' ancient hate. Such was his sickness . . .

The North Star Basin Mine was an old, deserted and, for the most part, totally forgotten working, crouched under the blunt nose of the extreme northern end of the Maacama Rim. There was a shallow shaft, long ago caved in, a close-to-the-surface drift now also just a collapsed tangle of rock and earth and the bones of rotted timbers, and one short stretch of open tunnel reaching some sixty or seventy feet back into the solid bulk of the rim.

Nature, in her endless patience, had gone far toward erasing this scar of man's past activity. The dump was covered with brush, and more of the same had pushed at the sides of the sagging mine buildings, wearing them down, covering them after they fell. Stray odds and ends of metal that had once been parts of the hoist machinery were now just thin streaks and patches of ocher-brown rust, fading a little more with each passing winter.

Also, long ago, Nature had brushed in the trail to the spot, and you reached it, not by any direct route, but by a process of seek and find, and unless you knew exactly where to look, then you did not find at all.

Some dozen feet inside the mouth of the open tunnel, Fitch Gentry had his blankets spread. A little to one side of the tunnel mouth was blackened fire stain and scattered ashes. Here, Fitch did his cooking. Here, if a man used only well-dried fuel, there was no risk of smoke betrayal to any searching eye. For what smoke there was, filtered up the face of the rim, spreading and thinning as it climbed, and by the time it reached the crest and so met the open sky, what remained was little more than a faint and quickly dissipated haze.

At the dark inner end of the tunnel, clear water trickled down, worked a way along the junction of wall and floor of the tunnel, finally coming into the full light of day to gather in a little catch basin just outside the tunnel mouth. So, if he possessed sufficient food, a man could make out well enough. Here was good water, solid shelter and comparative security for a hunted man. But Fitch Gentry hated all of it.

Hated it because he was alone. Because his bad leg had turned for the worse instead of for the better, hurting too much to tackle the long ride out of the valley by saddle. He hated it because while he had plenty of tobacco, and some food, he had no whisky. Because his bed, even though he'd gathered and spread a thick pad of dried duff beneath his blankets, held no ease for him. And finally, being Fitch Gentry, he was, as always, forlornly sorry for himself.

Sourly brooding, he cursed a lot of people, including any and all whom he felt had in slightest part contributed to his present condition and misery. Even his grim, rugged old father came in for a share of this.

What, Fitch demanded of the tunnel's cloistered silence, was wrong with the old fool's thinking? Driving his only son off the ranch over such a minor thing as giving your word and then not keeping it. When keeping it could conceivably hang you!

And Larribee! Now there was one jingo he'd really even up with, come some fine day. When the cards lay just right. Someday—when this damned leg was really sound again. If it ever was . . .

It was aching now and Fitch got up off his blankets, limped to the tunnel mouth and looked around. Afternoon was almost done, shadows gathering blue and misty under the rim. A little way out and south of the mine site was an acre-sized clearing in the brush. Here grew some grass, and here Fitch had his horse on picket. Now, more for the sake of having something to do rather than any regard for the animal, he limped to the clearing, brought the horse in to water in the little catch basin, then took it back to the clearing and changed the picket to a fresh area of the scanty grass.

After which, while not really hungry, he set about getting supper, this also offering a small break in the monotony. He had only a little in the way of food. Bacon, coffee, some stale biscuits left from the batch he'd mixed up yesterday, burned half black and soaked with bacon grease. He craved something sweet, like a can of "air-tights" swimming in thick, rich syrup. He sure hoped Boardy Samuels would include some in the store of grub he'd promised to bring. And a bottle of whisky.

When was Boardy due? Tomorrow, next day? Living like this, without a damn' thing to do but lie around, a man lost track of time, the days and nights running one into another until time was just a blur of nothing and you got so you paid it no attention, and pretty soon you didn't know what day was which. And didn't much care, either.

Crouched beside his fire, watching bacon sputter in the pan, Fitch showed a lank and wolfish look. His narrow face was patched and frowzy with dark whisker stubble, his eyes, squinting a little against the fire heat, smudged with sullenness and discontent. The grime of an over-all slothfulness stained him.

By the time he finished eating, twilight had come in across the land. He was twisting up a cigarette when he heard the muffled tump of hoofs. His first thought was that his horse had pulled its picket pin and was on the loose, and he lunged to his feet, struck hard with a saddleman's fear of being left afoot. A moment later he relaxed, for a call came drifting in from the outer gloom in Boardy Samuels' somewhat guttural voice.

"Ho—Fitch! All clear?"

Fitch answered with eager relief.

"All clear! Come on in, Boardy."

Boardy came ahead, his horse breasting through the sweep of brush. Fitch faced him, questions running eagerly.

"What's the word? You got any decent grub—or a bottle?"

Boardy shook his head. "No luck there. Ain't been able to get away long enough to get to town. I'll make another try tomorrow. Any coffee left in that pot?"

Stung with disappointment, Fitch did not answer. Boardy stepped from his saddle, hefted the pot, shook it. In the catch basin he rinsed the cup Fitch had used, drained the remnants of the pot's contents into it and drank greedily.

"This is a hell of a way for a white man to have to live," complained Fitch bitterly, hunkering down on his heels again. "I can't stand this place much longer."

"You won't have to," soothed Boardy, circling casually, a move which put him momentarily at Fitch's unsuspecting back.

Whereupon, coldly deliberate, Boardy drew his gun and shot Fitch between the shoulders. The impact of the heavy slug, from close up, knocked Fitch forward, face down, barely missing the fire coals. Boardy shot again, then watched for sign of movement.

There was none.

The reports had boomed heavily in evening's stillness, running huge and hollow up the face of the rim. Boardy lifted his head, keening the dusk with all his senses. He holstered his gun, went to his horse and rode off, striking south close in under the rim, leaving behind him a shocked silence in which a fire coal snapped in tiny violence, throwing a flicker of gray ash out to touch the cheek of the dead man lying there.

8

The afternoon was well run out and twilight closing thickly in, when Henry Jeffers brought his pack string swinging wide around the spreading mat of heavy brush off the north point of the Maacama Rim. Riding at a jog, the twelve mules of the string pressing faithfully at his heels, Henry was calculating the distance to the home corrals at Silver Ford and deciding whether to go on in tonight or strike over east to the Pride River and throw down a camp until morning.

An older man, weary of the saddle, might have decided on the latter course but, at twenty-two, Henry was full of youth's eagerness. Town was, he knew, a good three hours away, but even so he might get there in time to find the Rojas family still up. In which case, he'd have a chance for a brief visit with Rita. And just the sight of her, the sound of her voice and the warmth of her smile would, for Henry, more than make up for the extra effort of getting there. So he shook his rein, lifting his mount to a slightly faster gait.

It was something better than two years since Henry Jeffers, a tall, rawboned, deliberate young man, gifted with a patience that made him a born hand at handling horses and mules, had gone to work for Ira Redstone. He had started in as a roustabout and general handy man around the freight and stage corral, but his sober, straight-eyed dependability over others who couldn't leave the bottle alone, soon had him moved up to more important duties, even to occasionally handling a jerk line on a freight outfit over the long haul to and from Medicine Lake.

It was this same dependability that later caused him to be given the chore of running the supply pack string which Redstone sent out every six weeks on the wide swing that touched all the little, remote ranches scattered through the deeper reaches of the Sabines and across the wild country beyond the Maacama Rim. It took ten days or better to complete the whole swing and along the way Henry Jeffers left flour and bacon, beans, bags of green coffee, boxes of "air-tights," all sorts of staple provisions.

To young Henry, handling this pack string hardly qualified as work. He liked the movement and freedom of the trail. He liked his certain welcome at some distant ranch, where his arrival was a break in the isolation and the loneliness. There the womenfolk would touch up their appearance a bit out of respect for their visitor, and shy-eyed kids would come sidling, drawn by the lure of a piece of hard candy Henry always had in his saddlebags.

Then there were the menfolks, who would hang on his every word as he gave out with the little store of news items he'd been able to gather since his last visit. Henry knew these people liked him and depended on him, and looked forward to his arrival—which was a good knowledge to possess.

This, he reflected, had been a good trip. Every mule in the string, aside from the one carrying his blanket roll and frugal camp outfit, was heading home under an empty pack saddle. This morning, Mark Eaton, over past the rim, had taken the last sack of flour, the last side of bacon—which was another cause for Henry's satisfaction. He liked to feel that he'd given his employer honest effort for his wages.

Not that he intended going on forever as somebody else's hired man. Someday, he'd have a business of his own. Probably something in freighting and supply, for he liked that kind of work because, among other things, it had to do with horses and mules. A business of his own, to make the future solid for himself and—maybe—Rita Rojas . . . !

This was a thought that came to him more and more often of late. He had it in his mind now and was so lost in the warmth of it that at first the two sullen, half-smothered gun reports punched at the outer edge of his consciousness without particular significance. Then they registered fully, jerking young Henry out of the roseate haze of an intangible future to the solid realities of the present moment.

The shuddering echoes had come in from the right, over there beyond a long quarter mile or more of clotted brush and gaunt bull pines, where the darkening bulk of the Maacama Rim lifted against a sunset sky that had shed all its fire and showed only the faintest pearl gray afterglow to battle uselessly against the onrushing tide of night.

Henry reined in, the pack string coming to a jingling halt behind him, the mules bunching and crowding. He listened and looked, hearing nothing more and seeing nothing. For over there against the rim, dusk had become a dense, blue-black belt of shadow. He started to ride on, then reined back again, frowning in speculation.

This was pretty remote country, just here. He had been through here before, making the swing with the pack string, and he could not recall ever meeting with anyone in this exact area. What could two quick shots mean, at this late hour in the day? If anything? Or could they? Some poor devil, down and hurt out there, trying to signal for help, maybe?

Henry had heard it said that three quick shots, evenly spaced, was an accepted signal call for help. But just two shots—? Unless, in his abstraction, he'd missed the third one. . . .

Indecision held him, and, being the solid, purposeful sort that he was, he hated this. Abruptly he knew he'd have no peace of mind unless he made some sort of investigation. So he reined his horse into the brush, pointing for the rim. The pack mules lined out, following him.

The town of Silver Ford lay quiet under the comfort of another velvet-soft night.

Grant Hilliker now slept in Jim Larribee's bed in Hannah Virgil's cottage, soothed by an opiate Doc Shields had given him. Here he would know a greater quiet than in his own room in the Riverside Hotel, and here also, he would be close under Hannah Virgil's watchful kindly eye and ready to her capable nursing. They had carried him here from Abe Chain's harness room on a blanket stretcher.

With Hilliker resting quiet, Jim Larribee had gone to his office and remained there throughout the balance of the day. It had been a long day and he was low in spirit. The volcano of seething rage that had towered in him and made him club Curly Gibson down so mercilessly seemed to have burned dry some well of energy in him, leaving him slack and listless. The last food he'd eaten was the meager breakfast he'd cooked for himself on Concho Creek early that morning, and even now, at this late hour, thought of food was not in his mind until Rita Rojas came quietly through the office door, carrying a tray, which she placed on his desk.

"My mama," she announced simply, "says that you must eat, Jeem."

There was a big bowl of chili, another of beans, some tortillas and a jug of hot coffee. The moment the spicy fragrance of it all struck Larribee's nostrils, he was ravenous.

"Youngster," he said, "there are two angels in the Rojas family. You and your mama."

Rita assumed her favorite perch, on the corner of the desk, watching him gravely while he ate. Her usual wriggling exuberance and gaiety were missing. Glancing up at her, Larribee spoke between mouthfuls.

"Little old sober sides tonight. What's wrong?"

She touched a hand over her heart. "In here. I am not happy w'en my friends are in trouble."

"Friends?"

She nodded. "You, Jeem. And Mister Hilliker. Every time I think how he look w'en first I see him this morning, I cry inside."

"Doc Shields now says Grant will look as good as ever, one of these days."

"I know. But always, I think, I must remember w'at he look like once. And you, Jeem—they would take that off you." She leaned forward and laid a fingertip on his star. "Because w'at you do to that Curly Gibson, no?"

"Not just for that, youngster. For a lot of reasons, all dirty. But maybe we'll fool 'em." He straightened in his chair, shook his shoulders.

This hot and savory food was like a heavy jolt of liquor. It took hold inside, warming him. It put new vigor in him, quickening him mentally and physically. He showed Rita the shadow of a hard-twisted grin. "That's it, youngster—maybe we'll fool 'em."

"W'at you do, Jeem?"

"Just not let them take the star off me."

"Then they fight with you?"

"Maybe."

She propped her chin with one small brown fist and cogitated. "I do not like you fighting," she announced presently, strictly grave. "Someday you get hurt. I would let them have their old star."

"Not for a while, youngster. If I gave in now, they'd think I was afraid."

"And would that be so bad? W'y are men so afraid—to be afraid? It is nothing to be afraid. I have often been afraid. Like every time that Curly Gibson look at me, then I am afraid. I am glad that you beat him, Jeem. Is it wrong for me to be glad of that?"

Draining the last of the coffee, Larribee leaned back, wiped his lips and began rolling a smoke. He looked at Rita narrowly.

"If I'd have known Curly Gibson ever bothered you, I'd have hit him twice as often and twice as hard."

A flush stole through her soft, dusky young cheeks.

"W'en Hennery Jeffers looks at me, it is like a bird sings inside me," she explained with child-like simplicity. "But w'en that Curly Gibson look at me—!" She shivered. "Like that, Jeem—I am cold all over. I want to run and hide."

Larribee's lips thinned. "From now on he'll look the other way when you're around, youngster."

He stood up, stretched, feeling the need of movement and a breath of air.

"I'm going to see how Grant Hilliker is doing. Here, I'll carry that tray."

He did so, as far as the Rojas doorway. There, as he turned it over to Rita, he said, "Thank your good mama for me, little one. Tell her I said she was an angel."

This brought a giggle. "An angel, so fat, Jeem? She will laugh like I do."

Striding up Valley Street, Larribee was surprised at the new verve he felt. Probably, he reflected, when a man dropped deep into a depressive pit, he was bound to bounce back; action and reaction—something like that.

The night was good, one of a million stars, low swung and glittering against the vast black sweep of the sky. A little wind came down off the Sabines, cool and crisp and sweet with distance, to lay soft fingers about a man's face and fill his lungs with a vital essence.

There was light and some activity in the

Maverick Bar, but Larribee did not pause there. Across the street the Acme Mercantile building lay dark and sprawling, the porch, under the long run of its gallery, a belt of inky shadow. Larribee wondered if it was his imagination, or if the grotesque bulk of Big Dan Sharples was really slouched in a chair on that dark porch, brooding his equally dark thoughts and laying his dark plans. . . .

Hannah Virgil answered Larribee's guarded knock, and held a low-turned, shaded lamp for him. By the light of this he saw that Grant Hilliker was still sleeping but definitely better. It was, he thought, strange how bulk and substance seemed to have returned to the figure beneath the blanket.

"Doctor Shields will be in again in the morning," Hannah Virgil said, as Larribee was leaving. "Now how about you, Jim? Where will you sleep?"

"I'll make out all right," he assured her. "There's a fair to middling bunk in the back room of the office, by the jail." The white glint of a quick grin showed against the deep weathering of his face. "Been many a drunk slept it off on that bunk. We'll see how it holds up under a sober man."

Back at the office again, he'd just got a light going when the quiet of the street was broken by the massed shuffle of hoofs, the creak and jangle of equipment. Then it was young Henry Jeffers bursting in through the door, exclaiming with relief.

"Sure glad to locate you, Mr. Larribee. Was afraid I might miss you."

Larribee looked at him, wondering. He'd never seen this lanky, steady-paced young fellow so plainly upset.

"What is it, Henry? Something wrong?"

Henry drew a deep, gulping breath, then said flatly: "It's Fitch Gentry, Mr. Larribee. He's dead. Somebody killed him!"

Larribee jerked to full alertness. "What's that—what's that? Fitch Gentry—killed! How do you know?"

For long miles and hours, Henry Jeffers had been carrying this thing. Now it burst from him in a gusty flood.

"I heard the two shots. Something told me I'd better investigate, so I did. Then—then I found him. It was pretty dark, so I lit a couple of matches and I saw how it was. He'd been shot in the back—twice."

"Where was this?" Larribee demanded.

"Up in that wild country around the north end of the Maacama Rim. Near as I could tell it was where an old mine or somethin' of the sort had one time been."

"You say you heard two shots. You didn't see anyone around?"

Henry shook his head. “Nobody, Mr. Larribee. Nobody but—but him—Fitch Gentry.”

Larribee lifted his coat off a wall peg. “Can you find the place again in the dark, Henry?”

“Sure of it. You want I should ride out with you?”

“Guess you’ll have to, son.”

Henry wheeled to the door. “Be with you soon as I corral the pack string and saddle up a fresh horse.”

“I’ll be waiting at Abe Chain’s livery,” Larribee told him.

When Larribee turned up the street he noticed there was still a faint light in the kitchen of the White Stag eating house, so he pounded on the locked front door until Morrie Carr came, yawning and shuffling.

“Good Lord, Jim!” grumbled Morrie, when he saw who it was. “Can’t you figger a more reasonable time to think about food?”

“Not for me,” Larribee told him. “But for a kid who hasn’t eaten for probably eight or ten hours, and won’t have a chance for five or six more. So be a good fellow, Morrie, and throw a couple of heavy sandwiches together.”

“Oh, sure—sure,” growled Morrie. “Come on in. Only take me a minute or two.”

Leaving Silver Ford, Henry Jeffers gratefully consumed the sandwiches which Larribee had provided. After which, still stirred by the grim importance and equally grim excitement of his discovery, young Henry gave out with the whole thing once more, adding a few details he'd overlooked the first time. But this loquacity soon drained away, and they began riding the miles down in silence.

A little after midnight they crossed Concho Creek and headed on through the small, cold hours of the morning, each wrapped in the possessiveness of his own thoughts. On their left ran the Maacama Rim, its crest an edge of uneven blackness which one moment blotted out some of morning's chill and sinking stars, the next revealing them once more.

Beyond the distant Sabines, the eastern sky had begun to show a first faint paleness before Henry Jeffers drew a halting rein.

"We're close," he said. "If we cut over to the base of the rim here and follow along it, we can't miss."

They moved into the brush, pushing a slow way through it. In time they broke into a small clearing and yonder, at the far end of it, a horse blew and stamped a restless hoof. Alertly high in his stirrups, Larribee threw his curt call.

"Yonder there—name yourself!"

There was no answer, save the horse softly blowing again.

Larribee said, “Stay put, Henry. I’ll look at this.”

He rode forward and picked up the vague bulk of a horse swinging back and forth in a restricted arc. Understanding, he sent the word back.

“Just a lone bronc on a picket rope, Henry.”

Henry rode up. “Whose?” he asked. “Fitch’s, maybe?”

“Maybe. We’ll see.”

Larribee swung down, setting his heels hard against the earth to break up the saddle stiffness in him. He got hold of the picket rope and went along it, hand over hand, speaking easily. The horse quieted, and when Larribee ran a soothing hand down the curve of its neck and across its chest, gave out a gusty breath not unlike a sigh of relief. That same exploring hand moved along a somewhat ribby barrel to the near hip and down this toward the stifle. Here it paused, tracing the outline of a brand by feel.

“Star Cross bronc,” Larribee said. “Which should make it Fitch’s. We’ll take it along.”

Lonely, eager for company of its kind, the horse followed willingly at lead as they moved on, to come up finally close under the black bulk of the rim.

“Here,” Henry Jeffers said. “Right here.”

His senses probing and searching, Jim Larribee could smell the faint, scorched acridness of dew-dampened fire ashes. They left their saddles and prowled carefully. It was Henry Jeffers who presently dropped to one knee, then called up, his tone tired and subdued.

"I didn't dream it, Mr. Larribee. Here he is, just like I left him."

Larribee dug a stub of candle from a pocket, lighted it, and made grim examination. Henry Jeffers had it right. Fitch Gentry was certainly dead, and had been shot twice in the back, by a gun fired close enough to leave powder scorch on his shirt. Which, Larribee concluded, left but two possible angles to consider.

Either someone had got the drop on Fitch, held him still under their gun, then moved up close and shot him, or this thing had been done by someone Fitch knew well and trusted, and whom he was not afraid to have at his back. This last assumption, decided Larribee bleakly, made far more sense than the first. But there was a wicked ugliness in it.

Larribee straightened up. "We'll wait for daylight. There should be some sign showing."

It was a somber wait. Day, which could at times spread over the world so quickly, now seemed reluctant to bring a disclosing light to this spot. Yet the earth made its unvarying turn and the black, staining shadows finally began to thin and the fading stars scuttled wholly into hiding ahead of the ever broadening shafts of brilliance now lacing the eastern sky.

Things that lay close to the earth lifted and took on shape—like a dead man, and the frugal belongings that had been his. A saddle, propped against the base of the rim. A blackened skillet and an equally blackened coffeepot beside a campfire's cold ashes.

When the growing light outlined the tunnel mouth, Larribee investigated, found Fitch's blankets, brought one out to cover him. Then, frowning and intent, he began prowling and looking for sign. He found where a single horse had come in from the east, then had headed south, staying close in against the base of the rim.

He went back to where Henry Jeffers waited. Both of them would have welcomed hot coffee to drive out the chill and quicken their blood. Here at hand were the utensils and ingredients for its making, with fire fuel for the gathering. But these things had been the possessions of a man now lately dead, and they could not bring themselves to the use of them.

Larribee swung about restlessly. "We'll go now, Henry. We'll saddle his horse and take him in."

"Town?" asked Henry.

Larribee shook his head. "His home ranch. That is the way old Tasker will want it."

By the time they had Fitch blanket-wrapped, lifted and lashed across his saddle, young Henry Jeffers was very quiet and a pallor lay beneath the deep weather tan of his face. Observing,

Jim Larribee dropped a hand on his shoulder.

"I know how you feel, kid. This sort of thing is mean business. But you'll shake clear of it as we ride."

They headed south, close to the rim, following the tracks of the horse that had gone that way. But within less than a mile they lost these in a tangle of talus slides that had weathered down from the rim. So they swung out into more open country and angled through the shortest route to the Gentry headquarters.

They met no one. The early sun, drinking up the dew, brought with it a blend of earth's flavors to enrich morning's invigorating breath. Ordinarily, Larribee would have reacted to these fine, free things, but now he paid them no heed at all, walled in by the somberness of thought which held him.

It was, he decided, not so much the blunt fact of Fitch Gentry's death, for he knew Fitch's actual small worth as a man. But it was the manner of it, and the dark treachery it suggested, and what the impact would be on old Tasker Gentry. For, despite the fact that Tasker Gentry had equal hand in driving him off his Concho Creek holdings, and later bitterly fighting his election, Larribee could not help respecting the grim old cattleman. So it was that he had little taste for what lay ahead.

They came in on the Gentry headquarters

quietly. Two horses stood ground-reined in front of the ranch house. One was the trim little dun which Kelsey Fredericks often rode. Now, even as Larribee speculated on this, Tasker Gentry stepped from the ranch house, followed by John and Kelsey Fredericks. The latter two held back, but Tasker Gentry came quickly across the interval, his face iron-hard, his eyes, under tufted, frosty brows, full of a fierce blaze as they fixed on the blanket-wrapped figure and the horse which carried it. His words, spoken harshly, seemed wrenched from his lips.

"Last time I saw that bronc, Fitch was riding it. Now it's packing—who—?"

There was but one possible answer and Larribee gave it, simply.

"I'm sorry to bring him in this way, Mr. Gentry. But it is—Fitch."

He saw the gust of raw pain hit Tasker Gentry, hit and twist him for one bitter moment before being hidden behind an armor of steely will. Then the grizzled cattleman was rapping out another question.

"You?"

"Not me." Larribee's answer was curt, yet it held a real sympathy. "Not me—and I don't know who."

Tasker Gentry's glance was arctic bleak as he searched for the truth. He felt that he had found it and he nodded abruptly.

"You'd gain nothing by lying. Bring him in."

They moved carefully, keeping the blanket in place as they followed Tasker Gentry into the house with their burden. John Fredericks watched, gravely wordless as they passed. At his side, Kelsey was pale and very still.

They put Fitch on the bed indicated, after which Tasker Gentry turned and said:

"Give me a little time. I'll want all that you know."

They left him and moved out into the welcome sunshine again. Jim Larribee built a smoke, then turned as John Fredericks quietly spoke.

"You say you don't know who did it. Not even a guess?"

Larribee shook his head. "Not even a guess. Nothing about it makes sense."

The import of all that had happened over the past day and night, together with the long ride and lack of sleep, had drawn and hardened his cheeks and shadowed his eyes. He looked wolf-lean, and Kelsey Fredericks, watching him with sober directness, thought he looked older and more capable than she'd ever seen him.

It was a little time before Tasker Gentry came out of the ranch house, and then it was slowly, and with an old man's sudden weariness. He spoke to Fredericks.

"John, I want you to hear this with me. But it

may be ugly, and perhaps the lass—?" He looked at Kelsey questioningly.

She moved closer to her father, took hold of his arm. "I would rather hear it direct than secondhand," she said simply.

Tasker Gentry inclined his grizzled head. "You always did have courage." He turned to Larribee. "Now. Give me all of it."

Jim Larribee told it fully, but as tersely as he could, and when he finished, Tasker Gentry, after brooding a moment, put his glance on young Henry Jeffers and spoke almost gently.

"You were the one who found him, son? You heard the shots?"

"Yes, sir," Henry answered. "That's right."

"But you never saw or heard anybody?"

"Nobody, sir. When I heard the shots I was maybe five hundred yards from where I found Fitch. In between was a lot of heavy brush. And it was growing dusk then too. I wish I could help more, but I can't."

Henry Jeffers was very sober, straight-forward and sincere, and Tasker Gentry nodded gravely. "Anyway, son—thanks for finding him." Again the cattleman turned to Jim Larribee.

"Fitch was shot in the back, twice. From close up. There's powder scorch on his shirt. What do you make of that? You must have *some* idea."

"I've tried to figure it," Larribee said. "At first I thought of the Price Tedrow affair, down at Ten

Mile, and I wondered if maybe one of Tedrow's granger friends had somehow learned where Fitch was, and had set out to get even. But what seemed a much more reasonable angle—though a damned ugly one—was that this thing had been done by someone Fitch trusted and believed to be his friend; someone he wasn't afraid to have at his back."

"But who, man—who? And why?" Tasker Gentry's tone was tight.

Larribee shrugged. "That I have no answer to. No answer at all. Yet there must be one somewhere, and I'll do all I can to find it."

He turned to his horse, mounted, then looked down for a final word.

"If there is anything else I can do right now—?"

"Just find me the one who did it," Tasker Gentry said. "I make no claim to pride in Fitch as a man. Still, he was my son, and he was shot in the back, which is no death for anyone. So, find me the killer—"

Larribee settled himself in his saddle and went completely still, while he stared off across the valley. Then he turned his head to meet and hold Kelsey Fredericks' glance for a gravely direct moment. After which he lifted a hand to the brim of his hat and wheeled his horse away, with Henry Jeffers dropping in beside him.

9

Toby Dye was a faded, dried-up old rider whose best days were long buried in the past years. But he was a fixture at Star Cross. In the interests of the ranch he had suffered broken bones and shed blood. In the bunkhouse his bed was the one nearest the stove. At the long, oilcloth-covered table in the cook shack, his seat was always the one at the right hand of Tasker Gentry.

Gruff old Tasker, who understood the need for any man to hold onto some small morsel of pride, saw to it that Toby, while no longer able to stand up to the pound and drive of working cattle, still had enough mild chores about the ranch to keep him puttering, and so feel he was still useful.

This day, Toby was farther from headquarters than he'd been since the last time he rode to town, some four months before. Through the long-running shadows of sundown he moved into the bench and pot-hole country over toward the Maacama Rim. He was looking for the Star Cross crew, and it was well after dark before he found them, locating them by the glow of their campfire. He sent out his hail, then rode in and dismounted stiffly.

Boardy Samuels faced him. Boardy's eyes were shadowed, his tone faintly guarded.

"Toby! What the hell? This is a long way out for you. What's the idea?"

"Tasker sent me," Toby said. "Somebody killed Fitch!"

"Somebody—killed Fitch!" Boardy rolled up slightly on his toes. "How do you know?"

"Jim Larribee and that kid who runs Ira Redstone's pack string, they brought Fitch in at the ranch this mornin', tied across his own saddle. And—"

"You mean," cut in Boardy harshly, "that Larribee caught up with Fitch and killed him?"

"Didn't say that," retorted Toby crossly. "Didn't say that at all."

The long ride had wearied him and set an old bullet scar across his ribs to aching. He was hungry and thirsty and evening's first chill was biting in. He was anxious for fire heat, food and hot coffee. He would have moved toward these things, but Boardy caught him by the arm, swung him around.

"Goddamn it, man—don't be so casual! Do you realize what you just said? Somebody killed Fitch. What's the rest of it—the rest of it?"

Toby jerked his arm away.

"It can wait until after I've et. Fitch is as dead as he'll ever be, which is that! And Tasker, he wants you fellers to come on in, first thing in the mornin'. So there's plenty of time to tell all

I know. Don't be so damned spooky. Let a man feed."

They made room for him at the fire, brought him food and coffee. Then they waited for the old fellow to give them the rest of the story.

The news carried undeniable shock. But among these men, deep down, there was little regret concerning Fitch, for toward him they had known scant liking or respect. In this matter, their feeling was all for old Tasker.

Boardy Samuels forced himself to hunker down, build a smoke, and act as stoic as the rest. But behind the broad mask of his swarthy face and shadowed eyes, conjecture was racing wildly. How had this happened? How had Fitch been found? Where did this kid who ran the pack train—this Henry Jeffers—come into the picture? What? How? Where?

Food, coffee and fire warmth mellowed Toby Dye. He finished his third cup of coffee, sipping noisily, then brought out his old pipe, packed and lighted it, and set it to gurgling softly as he puffed in deep content. Conscious of his momentary importance and pleased by the fact, he let the tension of waiting deepen considerably before he finally took the pipe from his lips, spat into the fire and began his story.

"Seems this kid, this Henry Jeffers, he's makin' his regular swing with Redstone's pack string. He's comin' through that wild country up north, just after sundown yesterday, when he hears these two shots, over against the rim. He figgers maybe somebody is down and hurt and signalin' for help. So he investigates and finds Fitch layin' there, plenty dead. He heads on to town, gets Larribee, and they come back, load Fitch on his horse and bring him in to the home ranch. That's it, 'ceptin' that like I said, Tasker wants you boys home in the mornin'."

"The kid, Henry Jeffers, didn't he see anybody around?" asked Boardy Samuels.

"Way he tells it, he don't see nobody, he don't hear nothin' but them two shots," Toby answered.

"But who'd want to kill Fitch?" asked another listener.

Toby shrugged. "No whiter, better man ever lived than Tasker Gentry." Then, drily, he added, "But we're all men growed, and done with foolin' ourselves. So we know what Fitch was. Me, I've more'n once wondered why somebody hadn't killed him a long time ago, for he was just as mean and slippery as Tasker is square. Just a hell of a lot of people didn't like Fitch, not none at all. You fellers know that as well as I do."

"Which don't change the fact that he was Star Cross," said Boardy Samuels heavily. "And which makes this thing our concern, plenty! I'm heading home, tonight. Rest of you come on in tomorrow morning. Toby, you can bed down in my blankets."

This suited Toby perfectly. He'd had enough riding for one day. His old bones were crying for rest.

Boardy Samuels caught and saddled and rode off into the night, apparently on the home trail. But as soon as he was well away from camp he headed directly for town. His thoughts were jumpy and uncertain and the acid of a persistent fear kept rising in his throat. It had all seemed so simple and certain, the plan he'd worked out with Big Dan Sharples. And it had been more than easy to carry out his deadly part of the agreement. But now—now—!

How in hell had he missed seeing or hearing anything of young Henry Jeffers and the pack string? Of course, according to the way Toby Dye told it, Jeffers had neither seen or heard anything beyond the two shots. Or—hadn't he—?

Maybe he'd seen and heard a lot more than he let on. Maybe Larribee had him telling his story this way so as to throw everybody off guard, while figuring a trap. Maybe—maybe—!

Boardy cursed, roweled his already speeding horse to a still faster pace. Goddamn the maybes! They could drive a man loco, wondering and guessing.

In Boardy Samuels there lay slyness and a broad streak of cruelty. Also, a dark ruthlessness that was utterly callous where his own interests were concerned. But he was not intelligent enough to rationalize, and so master the uncertainty now boiling in him. Any emergency or crisis such as this, demanding more than what the purely physical could supply, made his mind fuzz up and caused him to flounder and bog down mentally. What he wanted now was counsel from Big Dan Sharples, and he was riding to get it.

He drove his horse hard, and it was slugged with weariness by the time he reached Silver Ford. The instinct of a wary animal, more than anything else, caused him to leave his mount at the edge of town and move cautiously in on foot along River Street to the Maverick Bar corner. There was light in the Maverick and the faint murmur of men's voices. But Valley Street seemed empty and quiet enough.

Crouching slightly, Boardy crossed Valley and went swiftly along the River Street side of the Acme Mercantile building, then cut around to the rear of it. When he saw lamplight forming its yellow squares at the windows of Big Dan Sharples' living quarters, he gulped his relief. He moved up to the door and knocked.

He had to knock twice before the door opened. Big Dan grunted in surprise as the streaming lamplight disclosed his visitor. Then he jerked his head and stepped aside. Boardy hurried in. The raw, sweet reek of whisky and the steamy breath of hot coffee filled the room. Big Dan had been mixing one of his favorite coffee royals, and a half-filled quart bottle of whisky stood on the table. Boardy caught it up and took a deep drag.

"All right! All right!" growled Big Dan as he closed the door. "If that's all you came to town for, you could have stopped at the Maverick. What's wrong with you?"

Boardy, replacing the bottle, came around, coughing a little from the bite of the liquor.

"Ain't—ain't you heard?"

Big Dan's hooded, suspicious eyes pinched down a trifle. "Heard what?"

"About Fitch."

"What about Fitch?"

"He's dead. I finished him, like you told me. But—"

"Fine—fine!" cut in Big Dan. "That's what we wanted, wasn't it?"

Boardy made a nervous, slashing gesture, sweeping his opened, stiffened hand across in front of him.

"Wait a minute! Wait a minute! It ain't all that simple. Let me finish."

Big Dan heard him out, his dry, heavy face darkening to a faint scowl.

"So that's how it was," Boardy ended. "Young Jeffers and his damned pack string would have to be coming through, right at that time."

"You should have been more careful," charged Big Dan. "You should have made certain no one was around."

"You think I rode in on Fitch's camp with my eyes closed and my ears plugged?" Boardy retorted. "That's thick country, there. Lots of brush. Besides, it was comin' on dusk. Things the way they were, you could ride by within a hundred yards of a man and never see him. Or hear him, either, unless he was deliberately settin' up a hell of a racket. So, don't blame me. I did what our deal called for. It was just the Goddamn lousy luck of it; just that thousand-to-one chance turning up."

"That thousand-to-one chance has hung more than one man," Big Dan reminded. He paused to let the significance of this remark sink in, thus practicing a pet theory. This was: if you wanted to keep a man crawling at your feet—particularly the thick-headed kind—keep him scared. He watched Boardy Samuels run a nervous tongue back and forth across his lips several times, before going on in a more mild and soothing tone.

"Don't let it stampede you. You had your share of luck too. You didn't see or hear young Jeffers and, if you've told it straight, outside of the two shots he didn't see or hear anything, either. Fitch is dead, which is no loss at all. Only thing wrong is that we can't tie Larribee in with the killing. He was in town all day yesterday and evening, up to the time young Jeffers must have come for him."

"How about me?" insisted Boardy uneasily. "You really think, Dan, that Jeffers is tellin' all he knows? Maybe he's coverin' up some of it."

"I think he's telling all he knows," observed Big Dan. "He's hardly the kind to play clever or cover up. For that matter, why should he?"

"Maybe Larribee is tellin' him what to say and what not to say," Boardy ventured. "Layin' some kind of trap for me."

Big Dan shook his head. "If Larribee had any idea you were the man, he'd be after you right now, all out. You're letting your imagination run wild."

"What do you think I should do?"

"Act like you'd be expected to act. Be upset over Fitch's killing and anxious to locate the man who did it."

"You mean I stay right on at the ranch, like usual?"

"That's it. Nobody but you and me knows who killed Fitch. Nobody will know, if you get rid of that spookiness and play your cards right."

Boardy looked longingly at the whisky bottle again, and Big Dan nodded his permission. A second big drag on top of the first warmed his belly and burned away the worst of Boardy's doubts and fears.

"What," he asked, "does this do to me and the sheriff's job?"

"Just delays matters a little," Big Dan assured him. "You went through with your end of the bargain. I'll go through with mine."

"Got to get rid of Larribee first," Boardy reminded. "How you figger to handle that, now?"

Big Dan was still for a time, staring across the room into some dark decision of the future. "There are," he said finally, harshness roughening his voice, "always ways and means. If necessary—the final one."

"Like Fitch?"

Big Dan nodded. "Like Fitch."

It was dark when Jim Larribee awoke. He lay for a little time, slowly dragging into fresh perspective the important fragments of the past seventy-two hours. In total, they represented more official activity than he'd known in any like period since pinning on the star. All the forming trends seemed to have suddenly fused and peaked up, demanding action and decision one way or another. He had made some decisions, irrevocable ones, which, he decided soberly, could have wide bearing and influence on his future.

He was on the old bunk in the back room of his office. He pushed up on an elbow, thumbed Durham and papers from his shirt, and built a smoke purely by feel. He lighted his cigarette with a sulphur match, then used the brief, sputtering glow of this for a glance at his heavy case watch. He blinked, startled at what the hands told him. After ten o'clock.

He swung his feet to the floor, fumbled around and found his boots and stamped into them. He got a lamp going and took another look at his watch, spurred by a faint feeling of guilt. When he hit the bunk after reaching town with Henry Jeffers, with a long, bitter day and an equally long, sleepless night behind him, he'd figured just to catch a few winks through the fag end of the afternoon, but with no intent to sleep this long.

He yawned, rubbed a hand across his face, felt the rasp of whisker stubble, so went through the discomfort of a cold-water shave. After which he had a wash and emerged from this wide awake, alert and hungry. He belted on his gun, got his hat, put out the lamp and went through the dark front office to the street. His hope was that there'd be a light still on in the White Stag, which would mean Morrie Carr was still up, baking bread or preparing some sort of food against tomorrow's need. Morrie might cuss and growl, but in the end he'd throw a little supper together.

There was no light in the White Stag. In fact, in all of town that Larribee could see, there were only three lights. In the corner window of the Riverside Hotel office, in the Maverick Bar and, way up Valley Street, a faint gleam that meant a lamp burning in Hannah Virgil's cottage.

It shaped up, Larribee reflected ruefully, as a hungry night. Unless there was something left on Tom Ivy's free-lunch shelf in the Maverick. At best, this would be scant fare, but better than nothing at all.

Along the open of the street the massed glitter of the stars laid a wash of thin, pale silver, which was more reflective glow than it was true light, yet it was enough to disclose a shift of movement over at the Maverick corner. To Jim Larribee it was as though he sensed, as much as saw this move, but because of its furtiveness it was enough to cause him to drop softly back until his shoulders were against the wall of the White Stag, and he was sheltered in a pocket of deep shadow.

The movement yonder resolved into the figure of a man, who now hurriedly crossed Valley Street toward the Acme Mercantile, slightly crouched, as though hoping this would enable him to elude observation. At the distance, in this tricky mixture of faint starglow and utter dark, identification was not possible. Yet Larribee knew a vague sense of familiarity.

The man had come up River Street and now, beyond Valley, kept straight ahead on River, presently fading into the shadow along the side of the warehouse end of the Acme Mercantile building. At the far back corner of this he showed again for a brief stride or two, then was lost in darkness again. Presently, beyond that back corner, a reflected glow of light showed briefly, then was gone. A door, decided Larribee, had been opened and closed. The man had gone into the back entrance of Big Dan Sharples' living quarters.

Had this happened a few nights ago, and had the man not shown that air of furtiveness, Jim Larribee would not have wasted a second thought. Now, however, with the grim portents of the past three days to consider, a thing of this sort could stand investigating. So Larribee crossed River Street and circled quietly to the rear of the Acme Mercantile. There was nothing to see, just a dark wall with two small, high-up windows framing dull lamp gleam beyond.

For a little time, Larribee stood there in the night, reaching for the identity of the man he'd seen. The fellow had been burly, somewhat resembling Curly Gibson. But it was strongly doubtful that Curly, after the physical going over he'd absorbed, would be up and around again this soon. Yet, if not Curly—who? Certainly not Ed Forbush, for the physical difference was too great. Maybe some other granger from Ten Mile? Possible, but not probable. Larribee shook himself. This was useless speculation and meant nothing. There was but one way to be sure: wait and watch.

Out here behind the Acme Mercantile was a

vacant area where old Charley Clark piled empty packing cases, kegs and boxes, and, at intervals, burned them. There was a sizable pile of them now, and against the dark bulk of this, where the mass of it would take him in and hide him, Larribee put an empty nail keg on end and settled down to wait and see this thing through.

He started to build a cigarette, but caught himself and let the pinch of tobacco sift away and the brown paper drift from his fingers. A glowing cigarette tip, a whiff of tobacco smoke across the dark, could betray a man's presence and position.

A gust of irritation swelled in him at the thought. It had become that kind of country, what with the dark currents of hatred and scheming flowing across it with ever broadening swiftness. It seemed, aside from a few exceptions, that a man could not be entirely sure of just who he might depend on.

This was high country, this valley of the Pride River, a land which the sun fully warmed by day, but also one where, when night came down, both the Maacama Rim and the Sabine Hills fed currents of chill across it. Right now, Jim Larribee wished he'd brought his coat along from the office.

Without it, he hunched his shoulders against the air's bite and decided that whatever the portent of this thing, he wasn't going to wait and watch too long—maybe half an hour. After that he'd get along and sample the comfort of the Maverick.

If only there wasn't that gnawing sense of familiarity to taunt him! That feeling that he'd seen the fellow before, some place—some time. Ever deeper grew his certainty of this, as did the certainty that it hadn't been Curly Gibson.

Time passed. Across the settled quiet of the town drifted the faintest of echoes, the yammer of a coyote's loneliness, distant to the point of being as much imagination as fact. More definite, more certain, was an owl's round, hollow booming that came up from some river covert. Night burned its chill against Larribee's cheeks, bringing with it the matchless flavor of space.

Abruptly, and centered between those two yonder windows, a door opened. Two men stood briefly framed in its rectangle of light. One was Big Dan Sharples. The other—and this fact brought Jim Larribee to his feet with a startled hiss of indrawn breath—was Boardy Samuels. No possible mistake, not at this distance and against that light. Boardy Samuels—!

The door closed. Boardy Samuels moved along the black shadow of the building and turned into River Street. Jim Larribee, following, saw Boardy cross Valley and vanish into the pale, cold starlight down the farther reaches of River Street. Presently, faint and quick fading, came the splash of hoofs crossing the ford.

Soberly, and with plenty to think about, Jim

Larribee went into the Maverick, where he found enough on the free-lunch shelf for a frugal sandwich. This, with a whisky toddy to drive out night's chill, was his supper.

From the Maverick, he returned to his office and, over a final smoke, reached for the significance of what he'd observed. So far as he knew, there had never been any friendship between Big Dan Sharples and Boardy Samuels. Certainly, as Tasker Gentry's foreman, Boardy was across the fence from Big Dan. Also, Big Dan was largely responsible for Boardy being an ex-sheriff, having fought him bitterly in the last election. Yet this night, the pair of them had met furtively. Why?

Again and again Larribee turned the question over in his mind. There could be, he decided finally, but one answer. Here again was the leering, foul face of the double cross. But working how and against whom? Was Boardy, while taking the pay of Tasker Gentry, selling him out to Big Dan? Or was old Tasker mixed up in it somehow?

This last thought Larribee discarded immediately. The past few days had convinced him that Tasker Gentry wasn't the sort to double-cross anyone for any reason. So left was only one conclusion. Boardy Samuels was selling his saddle, going over to Big Dan Sharples—for a reason that was any man's guess.

By the time he reached decision, Larribee's cigarette had gone cold. Tomorrow, he decided, he'd ride out to Star Cross. He'd get Boardy Samuels in front of Tasker Gentry and question him pointedly about tonight's little incident. One way or another he'd force the truth. With this conclusion, he turned in.

He was up early and took breakfast at the White Stag, then went along to Abe Chain's livery barn, saddled his horse and headed out and away.

It was a fine, vigorous morning, holding a crisp flavor that made a man think of autumn. It gave Jim Larribee a little start to realize that this season was just across the edge of the world, waiting its turn to move in. In fact, it was already breathing on the higher crests of the Sabines. Up there the aspen swamps were beginning to show as smears of gold tucked here and there in the blanket of evergreen conifers, while the crimson of the cherry brush was a warm flush of color under the rimrocks.

Savoring these good things as he rode, Larribee found that the grind of irritation he'd known since the showdown and open break with Big Dan Sharples had greatly lessened. Nothing, he reflected, could raise more hell with a man's peace of mind than uncertainty. He'd had his considerable share of this, but now had pushed it aside as decision and purpose clarified and steadied in him.

His defiance, flung in the teeth of the county commissioners, had been product of the gray and wicked anger that had seethed in him at the time. Yet, on sober reflection, no better answer had offered itself. For should he knuckle under to Big Dan now, Larribee knew he'd surely be done in the Pride River Valley. Here there would be nothing left for him, neither a share of the earth or the water or the confidence and respect of those who counted. And forever after, his own self-respect would be forfeit.

In his defiance he had flatly stated that he would continue to wear the star until the people voted it off him. These had been good words, stoutly spoken, stoutly meant. They were just as good and sound now as they had been then. So, until that day came, the star was his, and he'd wear it as it was meant to be worn!

The sun was well up by the time Jim Larribee reached Star Cross. For a moment he wondered at the seemingly deserted state of affairs. Then he saw them, a dark group of figures gathered on the crest of a little roll of rangeland that humped up some half mile east of the ranch house, before falling away in long, gradual slope to the river beyond. Besides people, there were a buckboard and a spring wagon out there and a number of saddle animals.

Immediately Larribee understood and he sent his horse out at a run, slowing to a jog and finally a walk for the last hundred yards. He swung down and left his mount with trailing rein, then moved quietly up to the edge of the group.

Yonder was the open grave, beside it the long, narrow mound of raw earth. Star Cross hands had just stepped back after lowering the blanket-wrapped body of Fitch Gentry into the grave. Now it was John Fredericks who stood, sober and stern of face, a small worn Bible in his hand. He began to read.

"Man born of woman . . ."

Jim Larribee's glance stole around the motionless group. Kelsey Fredericks was there, standing beside Tasker Gentry, one slim hand tucked into the bend of the old cattleman's arm. Her head was up, her eyes, glinting with moisture, fixed unseeingly straight ahead. Tasker Gentry's face was grimly stoic, eyes shadowed under his frosty, frowning brows.

Among the cowhands, awkward and inarticulate at moments such as these, was Len Hobart and a couple of other Fredericks riders. The balance were Star Cross hands, one of them Boardy Samuels, who stood holding his hat in front of him with both hands, his head, with its coarse bristle of hair, slightly bent, his broad, swarthy face expressionless.

Jim Larribee was remembering the man as he had seen him last night, furtively slipping in and out of Big Dan Sharples' back door. Last night's evidence cried out that Boardy Samuels was untrue, yet at this solemn moment he still stood as part of the Star Cross.

Fixedly, Larribee studied him. There was animal power in this man, with his heavy shoulders sloping down from a thick neck. From the side, in profile, his features showed a distinct cast of brutality. And his eyes, fixed on the ground, were black and glass-hard, unrevealing except for a pinch of slyness at the corners.

Feeling the pressure of Larribee's appraisal, Boardy stirred and turned his head to meet Larribee's eyes for a short, hard-staring moment. Then he looked away again.

". . . this we ask in the name of Jesus Christ, our Lord. Amen!"

John Fredericks' final words fell small and gentle under the sky's wide sweep. He closed his Bible and turned away from the grave, moving to join his daughter and Tasker Gentry, dropping a comforting hand on Tasker's shoulder as the old fellow slowly wheeled toward the spring wagon. Boardy Samuels clapped his hat on his bullet head and growled an order. Two Star Cross riders, shovels in hand, stepped forward and began filling in the grave.

Tasker Gentry's glance touched Jim Larribee. He spoke quietly.

"Good of you to show."

Larribee sought for the proper answer, was slow

in finding it. Tasker, understanding the reason for his hesitation, lifted a hand slightly and then let it fall away.

"It is done. There is an end to all things. Come over to the house if there is anything you have to tell me."

The old cattleman moved on. Kelsey Fredericks, slender and fine in the morning's sunlight, sought Larribee briefly with misty eyes, and to her he inclined his head gravely.

With her father, Kelsey got into the buckboard. Old Tasker climbed into the spring wagon where Toby Dye was already seated and waiting, and Toby kicked off the brake and swung the team away toward headquarters, the buckboard falling in behind.

Riders moved to their horses. Jim Larribee found Len Hobart beside him. Hobart was twisting up a cigarette. He nodded and proffered tobacco and papers, which Larribee accepted and spun up a smoke of his own. This gesture was Len Hobart's apology for things said and thought in the past. It was a satisfying thing, far more eloquent to Jim Larribee than any amount of words could be, and he knew a good inner warmth because of it. He and Hobart headed back toward the ranch house, riding side by side.

A rider came by, traveling at a faster pace than they, crowding Larribee to the extent of making his horse break stride and give way. It was a calculated, deliberate thing. The rider was Boardy Samuels and he drove right on without a backward look.

Larribee twisted in his saddle, the old fires flaring, angry words leaping up. They remained unsaid, however, checked by something he glimpsed clearly before Boardy drew too far ahead. And now the anger that had surged up in Larribee became a coldness that filled him with a bright, hard alertness and thinned his lips to a bleak line.

Len Hobart, who had noted the crowding but nothing more, said:

"He's a surly, arrogant brute. Hates you clear across hell, Larribee, for taking the star off him. A favorite trick of his, crowding a man. One of these days he's going to overdo it."

Jim Larribee drew a deep breath and his answer fell harshly.

"He just did!"

10

Toby Dye braked the spring wagon to a stop at the corrals, got stiffly down and began unhooking the team. Tasker Gentry stayed up on the wagon seat for a little time, his glance swinging out over corral and pasture, barns and feed sheds. It touched the wide acres of the range round about, then settled on the ranch house, in front of which John Fredericks had brought his buckboard to a halt.

Coming in with Len Hobart, Jim Larribee watched Tasker and thought that the old fellow had the look of a man who was measuring the results of his endeavor in life and finding them meager and unrewarding. For the son who should have inherited had proven poor metal, and now lay dead, back there where two men were about done with filling in the grave. So much, it seemed, for one man's lifetime of toil . . .

Slowly Tasker climbed down. With the earth under him again, he seemed to square himself, setting his feet more solidly. He straightened and growled an order to Boardy Samuels.

"Take the crew back and finish working out that country under the rim."

With steady step, Tasker crossed to the ranch house where John and Kelsey Fredericks had now left their rig and stood waiting. Tasker spoke to Kelsey and, as always when he addressed her, his tone turned very gentle.

"Lass, I think we could all stand a little coffee. You know my kitchen as well as I do. Would you mind?"

"Of course not," Kelsey said softly, turning into the house.

Tasker Gentry looked at John Fredericks, his long-time neighbor and friend. He sighed deeply and now his weariness showed.

"So I start over again, John. And I don't know why I should bother. Man is a fool to chase a big dream. There's nothing there when he reaches it. He just comes up with empty hands."

"No man's hands are empty while he's got a friend, Tasker," Fredericks said gravely. "Lot of good days ahead for you, yet."

Tasker considered this, his frowning glance again sweeping over this portion of his possessions. He dropped a hand on Fredericks' arm.

"I'm going to claim a small share of Kelsey, John. An occasional smile and word from her will mean more than ever to me, now. And all I got is going to her."

Tasker's eyes brightened as the idea took firmer hold. "Of course," he went on. "Of course. This ranch to Kelsey. That'll mean I've worked with purpose, after all."

Jim Larribee, along with Len Hobart and

the other riders, had stopped at the corrals. In Larribee, that hard, instinctive brightness of feeling had peaked up until his senses were humming like a taut wire. For after the first significance of what he had seen gave way to logical reasoning, conviction deepened and grew into utter certainty.

Len Hobart turned to the other two Fredericks riders. "We may as well pull out for home. Chores to do there."

Larribee spoke up quickly. "Hang around a little longer, Len. Things could get interesting."

Hobart put a narrowed glance on him. "Boardy?"

Larribee nodded. "Boardy."

"Not the time or place to go after him just because he crowded you," Hobart said curtly. "Been misery enough on this ranch for a while."

"I'm not going after him because he crowded me," Larribee said evenly. "This is something bigger than that—just a hell of a lot bigger. And the way Tasker would want it."

Hobart held Larribee's glance for a moment, then shrugged. "All right. I'll trail along."

Boardy Samuels had relayed Tasker Gentry's order to the Star Cross crew, and they began making preparations to head back to the bench and pot-hole range again. On some errand of his own Boardy went into the bunkhouse, which fact Jim Larribee noted with cold satisfaction. He was swiftly out of his saddle and moving toward the bunkhouse door, while giving Len Hobart low-voiced directions across his shoulder.

"Get Tasker and John Fredericks over here, Len. Make it quick!"

Puzzled and scowling, Len Hobart stared after Larribee. Then he shrugged again and headed to obey.

In the bunkhouse, Boardy Samuels hauled his warbag into view, delved into the tangle of its contents. He came up with a couple of sacks of smoking and a pint whisky flask, which still contained enough for a couple of good stiff snorts. He uncorked the flask and downed one of these.

Callous and brutally materialistic as he was, Boardy had found the burying business a little unsettling, though he couldn't put his finger on just why. Maybe it was because at the last minute that goddam Jim Larribee had shown up—and took to staring at a man like he might have had something on his mind.

Something Big Dan Sharples said last night had stuck in Boardy's mind, no matter how hard he tried to put it aside. About how one chance in a thousand could hang a man. Which was a hell of a thing to say, because it sort of pointed the finger. Maybe he hadn't been too damn' smart after all, making a deal with Big Dan. Maybe his eagerness to wear the star again had blinded him to the fact that Big Dan wasn't the soundest person to put trust in. For hadn't Larribee been Big Dan's fair-haired boy as late as a week ago? Now Big Dan was out to get him, any way he could.

Come to think of it, Boardy had heard some mighty shrewd men say that Big Dan Sharples had concern for a man only so long as he found him useful. The moment he ceased to be, he would be tossed aside without thanks or be-damned-to-you. Maybe that was what Big Dan figured to do with him. Maybe . . .

Boardy cursed softly. There they were again, those damned maybes!

He tipped the flask a second time, drained it, running his tongue around the neck of it to salvage the last amber drop. He tossed the empty container into the woodbox by the stove, where it struck solidly and broke with a thin crash.

The vagrant thought came to Boardy that old Toby Dye would cuss and growl around when he saw the shattered flask in the woodbox. Well, let him! He was like a fussy old woman about the bunkhouse, anyhow, always sweeping it out, always complaining if you threw a cigarette butt on the floor or left a stray sock or dirty shirt lying around. Anyone would think the damned old fool owned the place, instead of being plumb useless and kept on only because Tasker Gentry was too soft-headed to get rid of him. . . .

Boardy broke open one of the fresh sacks of Durham and built a smoke. He lighted this and sucked a heavy pull of smoke deep into his lungs, the comfort of it steadying him. Also, the whisky lay warm and soothing in his belly and he felt better all over, his doubts falling away.

What the hell! Fitch was dead and buried and there was no way anybody could connect him with the killing. Big Dan Sharples was the only one who knew anything for sure, and he'd keep his mouth shut. He'd damn' well better! It had been his suggestion, his idea all along about Fitch. Come right down to it, if anybody was mostly to blame for Fitch's killing, Big Dan was. Yes, sir . . . !

Swaggering a little, big-chested because of this somewhat obtuse whisky reasoning, Boardy clumped out of the bunkhouse, then stopped, dead still. Facing him was Jim Larribee. Half a step behind Larribee were Tasker Gentry, John Fredericks and Len Hobart. The latter three, though grave-faced, seemed openly puzzled. Larribee, however, was grimly purposeful and arctic bleak around the eyes. When he spoke, his words fell curt, blunt, each like a stone dropped on some ringing substance.

"A minute, Boardy! Something I want to ask you."

Some of Boardy's newly acquired certainty of security melted out of him. There was an instinctive animal wariness in him which kept him from showing this openly, except for a veiled flicker far back in his eyes. But inside him the whisky effect was suddenly gone, and his belly was cold. His parroted answer was flat, mechanical.

"Ask me—what?"

"First, about last night. What was your business in town with Big Dan Sharples?"

Jim Larribee let him have it that way, as direct as a fist in the face.

Boardy stared straight ahead. "I don't know what you mean."

"The hell you don't! Last night I watched you sneak in and out of town. You went into Big Dan's living quarters by the back way. I waited in the dark and saw Big Dan let you out again. The pair of you were on very good terms, from what I saw."

Behind Larribee, John Fredericks and Len Hobart had gone very still. Tasker Gentry, however, moved up beside Larribee, his fierce old eyes probing at his foreman, his words growling.

"Boardy, what's this he's saying? Were you in town last night?"

"He was in town," stated Jim Larribee flatly. "I saw him. And he visited with Big Dan."

Tasker Gentry's deep growl sounded again. "Well, Boardy? Yes or no? Speak up!"

Boardy's thoughts, now finally breaking free of the initial paralysis of surprise, caught a sly clarity. Further denial would be stupid and useless; the only way to handle this now was boldly.

"Yeah, I went to town and I did see Sharples. And—"

"Then why did you tell Larribee you didn't know what he meant? Why did you deny it?"

Boardy showed a flare of anger. "He's got no call to prod at me. It's none of his damn' business where I ride or who I see and talk to."

"It's my business," Tasker told him harshly. "When you ride for me and take my pay, it's plenty my business what you do and who you see. Why did you go see Sharples?"

"Because he sent for me. He sent Dobe Lear out to find me and tell me he wanted to see me."

"You didn't say anything about it to me."

Boardy shrugged. "No way I could at the time. You were here, at headquarters. I'm out with the crew, way over under the rim, working cattle. Then Toby Dye shows up with word about Fitch and I started for headquarters. But I got to figgering maybe I should find out what Sharples wanted. I thought, maybe, hearing about Fitch, he'd got a change of heart and wanted to call off this trouble that's been goin' on so long between him and you and Fredericks. Something like that. Whatever it was, I wanted to be able to give you the word."

"But you didn't. You said nothing about seeing Sharples. Why?"

Boardy began to flounder a little. "Well—I—you had a lot on your mind. Like what we just finished doin'."

"That is ended," Tasker said. "Now you can tell me. What did Sharples want?"

Boardy's hesitation deepened. Even playing it bold wasn't doing him any good. Seemed like the more he told, the more he had to tell. Now, to Tasker's last insistent question, what could he say? He was caught between fierce-eyed old Tasker on one hand, and the deal he'd made with Sharples on the other. Like he'd been herded into a trap. A blob of sweat formed under Boardy's hat brim, squeezed free and rolled down his swarthy face. His thoughts began to tangle frantically.

"What are you sweating about, Boardy?" The words were Jim Larribee's, and they were mocking, derisive. "Can't you think up the lies fast enough?"

Here was outlet for Boardy's badgered, trapped emotions. He turned, his head and heavy shoulders swinging, and his words fell thick and savage.

"Hell with you, Larribee! Lay off throwin' your weight at me! I don't recognize that star as anything, with you packin' it. I don't have to answer to you!"

"Wrong!" Larribee told him, all the first

remorseless, flinty drive back in his voice. “Answer me this, Boardy. What did you shoot at lately—shoot twice?”

Boardy’s restless, weaving swing became a graven stillness. His head slowly sank deeper between the heavy, mounded muscles of his shoulders. His eyes, as he stared at Larribee with the intentness of a coiled rattler, were all blank, surface glitter.

“That’s right,” Larribee went on. “Two shots. And if you didn’t want anybody to know about them, you shouldn’t be so damned careless about the little things, the kind of things that have hung more than one man. Boardy, just where were you the other evening when Fitch Gentry was shot in the back—twice!”

As he listened to these words, all balanced thought processes ceased inside Boardy Samuels’ head. The frantic tangle there became a complete incoherency. The jaws of the trap Boardy had sensed yawning about him were now closing in. He couldn’t figure how this had happened, but it had. And still, at the outer fringe of his mental chaos, he heard Jim Larribee pressing relentlessly on.

“Better come up with a good answer, Boardy. Else I’m taking you in, charged with murder!”

All the time he’d been throwing questions and charges at Boardy, Jim Larribee had been observing him with a taut and narrow care. He had watched the look of trapped desperation grow and grow, and he knew beyond all doubt that here he had his man. So now he threw a final dart, partly in the dark.

"Why did you kill him, Boardy? Did you shoot Fitch Gentry in the back because it was some part of a deal you'd made with Big Dan Sharples?"

Framing the truth so perfectly, these were the words that set Boardy off. And though he'd been watching carefully, ready for anything that came up, Jim Larribee was caught off guard, so swiftly did Boardy explode into action, dragging his gun. Larribee did the only thing he could do. He dove headlong at Boardy, smashing a shoulder into him, driving him staggering back.

Completely off balance after the impact, Larribee fell to his hands and knees. Boardy, his teeth bared in a snarl, pushed his gun forward and down, set to blast the life from the man on the ground in front of him.

But Boardy himself was still reeling from the impact, and the shift of his feet caught the low step of the bunkhouse. He tripped, falling sideways and back, through the bunkhouse doorway. He got a shot away, the report of it a flat thud of sound. But Boardy was falling as he fired, and the bullet he'd intended to drive slanting down into Jim Larribee's unprotected chest, flew high and wild.

Desperate as a fleeing animal, Boardy rolled and scrambled, lunging deeper into the shadowy depths of the bunkhouse. Jim Larribee, coming up off his hands and knees, went after him, slanting through the bunkhouse doorway in a fast, crouched leap, which put him into the corner to the left of the door, and with the squat, rounded bulk of the stove offering partial shelter.

At the far end of the room, Boardy Samuels whirled, his gun lancing a pale pencil of flame, the report charging along the walls and across the rafters in a round bellow of sound. From the doorpost at a height even with a man's chest, splinters scattered before the furrowing lead.

"Drop it!" called Larribee. "You got this one chance, Boardy. Drop that gun!"

Boardy's answer was a thick, panting curse and another shot. The bullet clanked into the stove, skidded off and chewed solidly into the wall beyond, missing Larribee by inches only. Boardy tried a fourth shot and a fifth, and these the stove caught and blunted fully.

Larribee tried once more, his voice a harsh echo. "Last chance, Boardy! Drop it, I say!"

Boardy dropped his gun, for it was empty. But this did not mean surrender. Instead, he shot out an arm, swept a Winchester rifle from wall pegs above a bunk. And the thin, metallic clatter, as he swung the lever back and forth, charging a cartridge from magazine to barrel chamber, told

Jim Larribee that this thing must end only one way.

Boardy was a thick, menacing bulk there in the shadowed depth of the bunkhouse and now, into the very center of that crouched bulk, Jim Larribee drove his first shot. He heard Boardy gasp, and he threw a second shot, knowing it went home too.

Boardy Samuels bent far over, then came forward three slow steps, heavy, dragging steps, leaning ever farther with each one. Something unintelligible muttered off his lips, then he lunged out head first and lay sodden and still on top of the rifle he'd been unable to fire.

After the trapped, battering racket of gun report in the confines of the place, short stillness came down as an almost aching pressure, broken only by the penetrating hum of a terrified bluebottle fly's wild circlings.

The sun-filled rectangle of the bunkhouse doorway darkened with the figure of Len Hobart. "Larribee!" he called. "Jim Larribee!"

"All right," Larribee answered, his tone flat and mechanical. "All right. But—he's down. I—I had no other out."

"Just so it's him, not you," Len Hobart said.

Now it was Tasker Gentry and John Fredericks who came pressing in, and back of them, drawn by the gunfire, a quick-gathering group of pushing, wondering saddlehands.

Jim Larribee slowly went the length of the bunkhouse, stood over Boardy Samuels, staring down at him. He needed no closer examination than this, and he turned and nodded bleakly as Tasker Gentry's harsh words fell.

"He's done for?"

"Yes. He would have it that way."

"Maybe he was smart," observed Len Hobart steadily. "I'd prefer that finish myself to a rope around my neck."

Tasker Gentry's voice broke a little. "It's hard to believe. He was my foreman—and Fitch's friend. I—I hope there's no mistake here."

"If he was innocent, he had nothing to worry about, no need to go for his gun and try and shoot it out," put in John Fredericks.

"Then he was a renegade," said Tasker bitterly. "A damned dirty renegade, taking my pay and selling me out to Sharples. Acting the friend to Fitch, then shooting him in the back. But why, in God's name? Why—why?"

"Perhaps," said Jim Larribee gravely, "we'll never know. If it was something entirely within himself, we'll certainly never know. If it was something that had to do with Big Dan Sharples, then we may."

"What gave you the hunch?" asked Len Hobart. "All of a sudden you seemed so sure."

"Two things," Larribee explained quietly. "Fitch was shot in the back, at such close range his shirt showed powder scorch. At the time he was on the dodge. Which meant that he was bound to be pretty much alert; certainly too much so to let any hostile person sneak up behind him to about arm's reach. So there had to be only one other answer, which I've said before. The man who killed Fitch had to be someone he knew, a friend—or rather, one he thought to be his friend; someone he wasn't afraid to put his back to."

Larribee paused, thumbing his pockets for smoking. Again it was Len Hobart who proffered the necessary book of brown papers and little muslin sack of tobacco. After a couple of deep inhales, Larribee went on.

"Boardy Samuels fitted such a part, yet I hadn't really considered him strongly until last night, when I saw him sneak into town to spend some time with Big Dan Sharples. That started me really wondering about him, though of course I had no real proof of anything, one way or the other. But it did make me decide to locate him and ask him some questions about this and that. Then, coming in from Fitch's burial, I saw something that somehow made me as certain about Boardy as I was that I was alive. Len, give me a hand; I want a good close look at his gun belt."

Together they bent over Boardy. Larribee's face was wooden as he straightened up, the gun belt in his hands. He held it so the filtered light from a bunkhouse window struck it fully. He studied it a moment, then nodded.

"It's what I saw when he crowded me, coming in. Take a look, Len. Here are two empty cartridge loops, with filled loops on both sides of them. The empty loops are still standing out, full and round. Within the last couple of days, these loops held cartridges, same as the rest. But within the last couple of days, Boardy Samuels fired two shots, and used the cartridges from these loops to reload."

Len Hobart, observing closely, nodded, a gleam of approval in his eyes. "Right," he said crisply. "Right as rain!"

Larribee turned to Tasker Gentry and John Fredericks, holding the gun belt out to them. Particularly he spoke to Tasker Gentry.

"There it is, sir. To me it tells a clear story. I hope it does to you, so there will be no doubts."

"No doubts," Tasker Gentry told him. "Only a fool would try to go against such clear logic. And, like John said, if he'd been innocent, he had nothing at all to fear. His own actions proved his guilt."

The old fierce gleam was again in Tasker Gentry's eyes. He turned to the silent, staring members of his crew, grouped there at the bunkhouse door. With a hard jerk of his head, he indicated Boardy Samuels' inert figure, and his order fell harshly.

"Take him out of here. He was a damned foul, treacherous renegade. Take him out of here!"

Moving into the open sunshine, Jim Larribee crossed to his horse, hooked the near stirrup over the horn and began fussing with the latigo, which move was one of sheer pretense, for there wasn't a thing wrong with the set or tension of that latigo. But there was a cold and bitter tension inside Jim Larribee, for now the smothering bleakness of inevitable reaction had set in.

Now, over and over, he was living the wicked, wild moments in the bunkhouse. Again he was facing the savage desperation that boiled out of Boardy Samuels until it was not unlike the thick, musky odor of some trapped animal. Again he was hearing the hammering bellow of gun report, condensed by the confines of the room to a force that shook a man's heart and pressed his eardrums to a vibrating ache. And the solid thud of pistol lead flattening against the heavy iron of the stove, or skidding off this to splinter the wall beyond. All of these things, minor in themselves, but part of a wide-awake nightmare that kept haunting a man.

Worst of all, of course, had been the staccato, breathy gasp by Boardy when that first slug took him, and then, after the second bullet dug into his vitals, the way he had come forward those few leaning, dragging strides before toppling out on his face. . . .

Beside Larribee a man cleared his throat. It was Len Hobart, and he spoke gruffly.

"I know how it is, Jim. These things never end with the final gun. A man lives them over and over, each following time worse than the actual shootout. And then one day it's all gone away and you're a whole man again, with everything right and in balance again. Because you did only what you had to do. You gave him his chance. Not your fault he elected to go for the gun."

Larribee turned, met and held Len Hobart's solid, steady glance. He nodded, drawing in and letting out a deep, slow breath. His shoulders lifted.

"Thanks," he said. "Thanks, Len."

"Yeah," said Hobart again, "I know how it is. First inclination is to get off by yourself, to hide. But that don't do a bit of good. You can't run away from the world and you can't run away from people. Least of all can you run away from yourself. So you face up to the facts and be done with them, once and for all. Now there's hot coffee waiting over at the ranch house, and I know it sounds like a hell of a suggestion at a time like this. But old Tasker is having some, and he just buried a son. So—?"

"Of course," Larribee said steadily. "Of course."

He dropped a hand on Len Hobart's shoulder and they crossed to the ranch house together.

11

Approximately half an hour before sundown, Ira Redstone swung away from his freight and stage corrals and left Silver Ford by buckboard along the road to Ten Mile. Within the next quarter hour, two of his big Merivale freight outfits rumbled out of town along the same route. On the box of the first of these was a leathery old-timer, Joe Lollard. At the jerk line of the second was young Henry Jeffers.

Henry was wondering about things, because it was unusual to start on a freighting job at this time of day, what with sunset, dusk, then darkness scarcely an hour away. He had no idea where he and Joe Lollard were heading or why. He'd asked Ira Redstone about this when his employer first ordered him to harness up a string of mules, but Redstone said he'd be out ahead in the buckboard, and that he'd pick up the freight outfits along the road and guide them to their destination.

Not that Henry minded the prospect of extra work, even though he'd already put in a full day around the corrals, where there was always plenty to do, caring for livestock, greasing and repairing wagons, cleaning and soaping harness and a hundred other minor but necessary chores.

Nor had young Henry pounded out enough monotonous, unrewarding miles on the box of a toiling, jolting freighter to have become calloused and ingrown and indifferent, like, for instance, crusty Joe Lollard. Instead there was still enough boy in him to exult in the feeling of power that came to him with the knowledge that his was the sole responsibility and guiding hand over these tons of wagon rolling and creaking under him. Also, that line of sleek mule backs strung out along the chain ahead—he always knew a little thrill when a shouted word, or a twitched signal on the jerk line, set that living mass of flesh and power answering to his will.

A quickening breeze was streaming across the valley from the west, and Henry was thankful for this too, for it caught at the clotted dust the moment grinding wheels and plodding hoofs slashed and scattered it, whisking it away before it could lift, so that up on the wagon box the air was clear and clean. But Henry could recall times along this selfsame road on a dead still day, or with the breeze a following one, when wagons and mules moved constantly in a clinging, amber shroud of dust so punishing that, to breathe at all, a man had to tie a bandanna handkerchief across nose and mouth.

Here, where the road ran straight and level, a man need do nothing but ride, confident the mules were certain in their knowing and doing.

And, Henry had found, the best way to endure such miles was to set your thoughts free and reaching. Which he now did, and because of his part in it and because it was such a recent thing, he again reviewed the shooting of Fitch Gentry and the known facts surrounding it.

A twist of feeling went through him on recollecting the emotional jolt he'd known when he first found Fitch's body, and then later, how it had affected him when he helped Jim Larribee load that same stiffened body on a horse. He had, reflected Henry in rueful soberness, emerged from that experience somewhat older than the few intervening hours warranted. . . .

For the life of him, Henry could not imagine how one man could shoot another in the back the way it had obviously happened to Fitch. Nor could he, recalling those he knew, think any of them capable of the act. This went to prove Henry Jeffers a singularly sound and uncomplicated young man.

He doubted strongly that Sheriff Jim Larribee would ever find the guilty man; there was so little to go on. He was sorry about that, not only because he wanted to see the guilty one brought to justice, but because he so deeply respected and admired Jim Larribee. And, Henry admitted in silent uneasiness, there was some talk going around that Big Dan Sharples and the other two county commissioners, Ira Redstone and Bert

Carter, had decided Larribee was not doing his full duty as sheriff, and were going to replace him. This move, Henry decided, with a little surge of anger, would be a mighty dirty deal.

Henry did not know Big Dan Sharples too well, never having had occasion to be around him or have anything particularly to do with him. A time or two, Henry had put a freight outfit up alongside the Acme Mercantile, there to deliver a load of supplies he'd just brought in from Medicine Lake. At such times, Big Dan worked with Charley Clark, checking these off against the invoice. But he never paid Henry much attention or had much to say to him, and Henry, liking most people, knew an instinctive repulsion for this ungainly man with his heavy, domineering features and hooded eyes. Most certainly, Henry vowed, he'd take Jim Larribee to Big Dan Sharples, a thousand times over. . . .

The sun, after sketching a fifty-yard-long shadow of the freighter, now dipped behind the distant Maacama Rim, and right away the air grew cooler and the mules felt the difference and stepped up the pace of their own accord. Even so, decided Henry, if he and Joe Lollard were headed for Ten Mile, it would be well after dark before they got there.

It wasn't Ten Mile. Just before dusk became full dark, there was Ira Redstone in his buckboard, waiting at the turnoff of an old and seldom-used road, which Henry had noted before, and often wondered where it led to. Apparently he was to find out this night, for now Redstone swung his buckboard into it, and Joe Lollard followed with his freight outfit.

Ira Redstone had been alone in his rig when he left Silver Ford, but he wasn't now. Somewhere along the line he had picked up a companion, and though Henry Jeffers, from this distance and in the thickening dusk could be sure, he thought the fellow on the buckboard seat with Redstone looked like a granger from Ten Mile whom he'd heard named as Forbush.

The old road angled out across the valley toward the darkening mass of the Sabine Hills, and presently began to climb at a long slant. Little used and weather rutted, the way was rough, and Henry had a small time of it, balancing to the lurch and jolt and swing of his wagon.

As the miles crawled by the road steepened, and ran into the twists and turns of a sheer-sided gulch leading ever deeper into the hills. In time they climbed out of the grass country into brushland, and from this finally into timber, where presently the road began running almost level again, though Stygian dark. Henry Jeffers was thankful that Joe Lollard was leading the way, making his own skinning job easier and surer.

Presently the timber thinned and the road led

out into a stretch of open, where the stars cast a glow that was white and revealing after the gloom under the timber. And here, abruptly, Henry Jeffers heard sheep and smelled them.

Ahead, Joe Lollard's wagon came to a halt, and Henry leaned into his own brake strap. He couldn't see the sheep, but the complaint of their bleating lifted in a thin overtone of steady protest at a time when they should have been bedded down and quiet. Henry wondered about this.

Ira Redstone called an order to Joe Lollard and Lollard's wagon creaked ahead and swung off the road out into the flat of this starlit mountain meadow. When Henry would have followed, Redstone stopped him.

"Not ready for your wagon just yet. Leave it here and come bear a hand."

Out there in the meadow was a small, flimsy, brush-sided corral, thickly jammed with complaining sheep. Under Redstone's directing, Joe Lollard pulled to a stop beside this, then went to work at the tail gate of his wagon. Grouped at the rear of the wagon besides Ira Redstone and Ed Forbush—now that he was close enough for sure recognition, Henry saw that it *was* Forbush—were three other men. Two were squat, powerful Basque sheepherders, the third a rough-voiced fellow whom Henry heard Forbush call Kincheloe.

As soon as Joe Lollard had the tail gate of his

wagon clear, the two Basques stepped into the corral, caught up a kicking, bleating sheep and lifted it across the low fence, where in turn Ed Forbush and the man Kincheloe grabbed it and swung it into the open end of the wagon.

"Get in there with Joe and keep the woollies shoved well up to the front end," Redstone told Henry. "We're going to have to pack the brutes tight to get them all in the two wagons."

The hot, acrid odors of the animals lifted thick about Henry and his hands grew oily and slick from grabbing and pushing at them. The work went steadily on until the wagon was loaded and the tail gate back in place. Then Joe Lollard moved his outfit ahead and Henry brought up his wagon. By the time the bed of this was jammed tight with sheep, the corral lay empty.

Almost immediately the two Basques disappeared somewhere into the night. Redstone and Forbush and the man Kincheloe gathered about the buckboard, their voices carrying up to Henry Jeffers as he climbed to the box of his wagon and donned a denim jumper across his sweating shoulders.

"The woollies will be damned glad to hit water," Kincheloe said. "We been holdin' them here for two days without any. That's why they're so noisy."

"Let's get rollin'," Forbush said. "Concho Creek is considerable of a drag from here.

Shack, I'll ride the lead wagon, you ride this one."

Ira Redstone called up to Henry Jeffers. "Until you and Lollard get rid of your loads, you take orders from Forbush."

Saying which, Redstone stepped into his buckboard and rattled off. Shack Kincheloe climbed to the box beside Henry and built a cigarette. He snapped a match alight and held it in his cupped hands while the flame grew, peering past this at Henry with pinched eyes. Then, as he tipped his head and lifted the match flame to his cigarette tip, the little bomb of light brought his face into momentary clarity.

Henry Jeffers was in no way impressed with what he saw. Shack Kincheloe's features were narrow and predatory, his mouth a thin-lipped gash above a flat chin. And as though he sensed Henry's instinctive aversion, his reaction was harsh and abrupt. He put the match out by whipping it from side to side, then flipped it away with a snap of his fingers, and his voice fell rough.

"I got a stake in this deal, so you'll take orders from me too. Just remember that, in case you start gettin' ideas."

"What ideas would I get?" retorted Henry.

"I wouldn't know. Only—don't!"

From the doorway of his office, Jim Larribee had seen Ira Redstone leave town in his buckboard, to be followed a little later by the two freight outfits, and, as Henry Jeffers had done, he too spent a little time pondering the reason for such activity this late in the day. Then he put the matter out of mind and left the office, heading up Valley Street toward Hannah Virgil's cottage.

When he let himself into the room that had been his, Grant Hilliker's voice, a little weak, but with the same old half-serious, half-scoffing tone, greeted him.

"About time you were coming by to say hello. Things change, don't they, my friend? Last time we were in this room together it was you who was using the bed, somewhat the worse for wear. Now I've taken over the role."

Larribee crossed over and looked down at this man he liked so well. To a considerable degree, normalcy had returned to Hilliker's face, though it was still deeply smudged with the savage black and blue of deep bruises. Out of these disfiguring shadows, however, his eyes glinted with the old dry humor.

"Bet I look like hell, Jim?"

"Not half bad compared to what you looked like a couple of days ago," Larribee told him. "Must say it does me good to see you coming along so well. Maybe you don't realize it, but you sure had some of us damn' well scared for a time. I'm wondering now if you should be talking."

"If I don't, Jim, I'll go stark raving crazy.

Hannah Virgil is surely one of God's chosen women, but I think she takes a small delight in bossing all hell out of a man when she's got him in a sick bed. Just the same, I got her to tell me a little of it, and Doc Shields told me some more. But it was Tom Ivy who stopped in for a couple of minutes this morning and gave me the part that really counts. It's about you, Jim, and it sure makes me happy."

"Curly Gibson," Larribee said, "will think twice before he tries another . . ."

"No—no!" cut in Hilliker. "I wasn't even thinking about Curly Gibson. He's just a blind, stupid brute who acted under orders. What I meant is that you really had your good look at Big Dan Sharples, that you caught him in his lies and deceit, and that you told him off and now you are where you should be and where I've wanted you to be right from the first. Your own man—completely! That's why I'm happy, Jim. And if by absorbing a beating I helped bring it all about, then the price was cheap—cheap!"

"You," said Larribee, covering his feelings with gruffness, "are a blasted reformer, a tub-thumper, a Messiah." Then he added, with a grim smile, "From what Big Dan said, I won't be carrying the star very long. The county commissioners are set to take it off me." Larribee paused to spin up and light a cigarette. "They've the right to do that, Grant?"

"Providing, and if they can actually prove real and adequate cause. But that 'if' can stand pretty high. In fact, I think I can make it so damn' high they'll choke to death trying to climb over it. I wouldn't worry about it," Hilliker said.

"I'm not going to," Larribee said. "But I might take the star off on my own accord. It gets pretty heavy at times."

Grant Hilliker pushed up on one elbow, the move dragging at stiffened muscles and making him grimace with pain. He exclaimed bruskly:

"That's no way to talk. Is it because of something that's happened which I haven't heard of?"

"Partly," Larribee said. Then he told of it all, giving out with the blunt, unadorned facts. "The thing that really sickens me," he ended, "is that any human being could turn as low and foul as Boardy Samuels. If human nature can creep around in slime like that, I'm not sure I want any part of a job that brings me in contact with it. Cattle are far cleaner and more reliable. For a time I knew some regret over having to gun Boardy. But no longer, now that I've thought it out. You know, Grant, I can see where this sheriffing job can not only turn into a damn' lonely one, but how it can put a rough, tough rind on a man."

Grant Hilliker lowered himself on his pillow again, staring thoughtfully up at the ceiling, now darkening with the shadows of sundown.

"You must look at it this way, Jim. Carrying the star means acceptance of a code of behavior that subjugates self to duty. At least that is the theory of it. The man with the star must see himself as an impersonal instrument of the law. Because, acting in the interests of the law, he's bound to contact much of life's ugliness and he must achieve a philosophy which completely separates real self from official self. So then he can walk through the slime and emerge untouched."

Larribee, driving a thin line of blue smoke from pursed lips, nodded.

"I've been trying to figure something like that. You clear it up pretty good. Maybe it's something a man has to sort of grow into."

Hilliker, his keen mind stimulated and racing by what Larribee had told him, now broke off in another direction.

"Jim," he said flatly, "it comes to me that Big Dan Sharples could be some way tied in with Fitch Gentry's death."

Larribee nodded again. "I've gone over that," he admitted. "But I can't figure why Big Dan would want Fitch killed. I can't see what he could hope to gain by such a thing."

"Try starting at the other end," Hilliker said. "Like this. Why should Boardy Samuels want to shoot Fitch in the back? Only one answer makes logical sense. Because he was to receive a reward of some sort. And who would be offering that reward?"

Larribee considered for a time in silence, then shrugged. "It's your question, Grant. You answer it."

Spurred by the possibilities of his thought, Hilliker came up on one elbow again.

"Don't tell me you're still hanging on to any lingerings of liking or respect for Big Dan? You admit you saw Samuel's sneaking in and out of Big Dan's living quarters. Doesn't that narrow the field pretty damn' well?"

"Yes," said Larribee, "when you put it that way, I suppose it does. Yet it brings us right back to the first why. Why should Big Dan want Fitch dead? Give me a good answer to that, and I'll go along with you."

Grant Hilliker's eyes squinted with thought as his lawyer's mind reached and speculated.

"Jim, if ever there was a man full of dark and devious purposes, it is Big Dan Sharples. And he is so consumed with hate and bitterness it is almost impossible for a normal person to understand how his mind works, or what is brewing in it."

"Once you said his big hate was for John Fredericks," reminded Larribee. "And that all he held against Tasker Gentry was that he happened to be Fredericks' good friend. Frankly, I doubt that Fitch was important enough to really count, no matter how you look at it."

Again Hilliker dropped back on his pillow.

"There's a steadfast streak in you, Jim," he said. "Once you cast your allegiance with a man, you don't let go of it easily. In one way, that is an admirable thing. In another, it could be your greatest weakness, and end up doing you deep harm."

Larribee took a final drag on his cigarette, then pinched out the butt. He looked at Hilliker with a faint, twisted smile.

"If you're hinting I have some regard left for Big Dan Sharples, you're wrong, Grant. I haven't. Not a shred. It's just that I don't want to let my official judgment be stampeded by my personal feelings."

The inner door of the room opened and Hannah Virgil came in with a bucket of steaming water and several towels.

"Time to work on the bruises again with hot compresses," she announced briskly. "And time for you to be on your way, Jim Larribee. Don't think you got in here without me knowing it. But I knew the only way to keep this man reasonably quiet in bed for another twenty-four hours was to let him get some of the talk out of his system. Now he's done it. So—out you go!"

Hilliker grinned. "There you have it, Jim. Didn't a wise man once say something about the hand that rocked the cradle ruling the earth?"

"Now that you mention it, I believe he did," Larribee said drily, moving to leave. "And thereby proved himself one smart son-of-a-gun."

Outside, evening was settling a blue autumn haze across the town. Moving downstreet, Larribee stopped at the White Stag for supper. After this, with a cigarette going, he went on toward the office. In front of Ysidro Rojas' place a saddle bronc stood, a shadowy bulk in the night's early starlight. Larribee gave the animal a moment of idle speculation, then turned into the deep full darkness that lay beyond his office door.

Instantly he stopped, for a delicate thread of perfume touched his nostrils, and then it was Kelsey Fredericks' voice that came to him.

"Jim—Jim Larribee?"

"Right! Girl, what brings you here? Something wrong at the ranch?"

"Yes—and no. Please, no light. We can talk in the dark, can't we?"

"We could, but we won't," Larribee said.

He scratched a match and lighted the lamp on his desk. As the flame of this swelled to fullness and the glow of it spread, it brought her from a voice in the dark to full physical reality. She was slim and straight in a divided skirt, a beaded, snugly buttoned buckskin jacket, and with a silk muffler at her throat. She was, he thought, always fair to look at, but there were times, like now, when she was cloaked in sheer, stirring beauty.

"You needn't be afraid to be seen with me," he said gruffly. "My friends tell me I'm a man of greater honor now than I was that night when we rode in across the hills from Soldier Creek, and you slept with your cheek against my shoulder."

She flushed warmly, but her glance held steady. "Perhaps," she said quietly, "I was considering you, not myself."

"How would that be?"

"You've been accused of being too friendly with Big Dan Sharples. I wouldn't want people to think I was trying to influence you too far in the opposite direction. And if my being here at all is disturbing you, as the tone of your voice seems to indicate, then I'd better leave." She started toward the door.

"No! Wait!" Larribee's protest was quick. "I'm sorry. Now why the devil am I always growling at you? When you're the one person in this world I'd never want to be surly with! Maybe it's because I worry about you that I want nothing to hurt you, ever! And if you happened to be seen slipping in and out of this office in the dark, people could be at their damned talk . . ."

She studied him for a moment, her eyes shadowed, while the tautness that had begun to pull at her lips, softened to the faintest of smiles.

"People will always talk, regardless. But I do find your concern comforting."

"You're not here without good reason," Larribee said. "What's wrong?"

"It's Dad," she said, now fully grave. "Today, when we got home from Star Cross, he was very quiet. When I happened to pass his room a little later, he was sitting in a chair by the window. He had a gun in his lap and he was oiling and cleaning it. It was a big, black revolver that has hung on the wall of his room for as far back as I can remember. There have always been a lot of guns of one sort or another around the house, but this one on the wall seemed to be something special. I know that one day, several years ago, I asked him why he kept it where it was. He said because it was an old and trusted friend, one that had in past years solved a lot of problems for him."

She paused, caught in big-eyed thought, and drew a deep breath before going on.

"I've always felt I knew my father thoroughly, that I certainly knew his moods. Now I found him in one I'd never met with before. It was as though he'd moved far away from me and was standing all alone at some great distance, behind a wall of bleak decision I just couldn't get through. It frightened me. I asked him why he was cleaning the old gun. His answer was that the old ways were best, and that by using them a man could settle things right, once and for all. Jim, do you know what he meant?" She finished with an anxious, breathless little rush.

Larribee nodded gravely. "I think I know exactly what he meant."

"He's going after Big Dan Sharples with that gun, isn't he?"

"I think that is what he intends. He told me he would if Big Dan kept forcing the issue. I know he had a final try at talking peace with Sharples and that it did no good. I'd say your father probably feels—and perhaps rightly—that Sharples is in some indirect way responsible for Fitch Gentry's death, which has been a hurt to old Tasker, your father's best friend. And, in turn, that led to the Boardy Samuels affair."

As he said this last, Jim Larribee held Kelsey Fredericks' eyes very directly, striving to see if his words stirred some revulsion in her—and afraid that they might. But he saw nothing except a thin tinge of pallor seep through her cheeks.

"Len Hobart said it could so easily have been you, instead of—of Samuels. Len said he doesn't know yet how you got by without being hit. . . ."

"And you don't hold it against me?"

"Hold it against you! Why on earth should I? You did only what you had to do; you had no other choice."

"Then," said Larribee, "we will see it only as something that is finished, done with, closed out. And so forget it while we put our thoughts on something important. About your father, I'll head him off."

She came swiftly close to the desk, faced him across it.

"Jim, you've got to! Because he'll go alone; he'd never ask anyone to share the risk with him. And Sharples has those two, that Dobe Lear and Curly Gibson. They'll gang on him, su—surely." She choked up, lips twisted and quivering under the hurt of thinking what could surely happen. She blinked, her eyes shining wetly as she looked at Larribee. "With you wearing the star, I've the right to ask this of you, haven't I?"

"Of course. Where is your father now? Has he any idea you're here?"

"No. I didn't leave the ranch until after he did. He went over to Star Cross again. Tasker Gentry had asked him to come back this evening. They were to decide on some kind of business, so Mr. Gentry said. I'm sure I know what that business is. It has to do with me. The two of them are arranging for my future, should anything happen to either of them. It is just the sort of thing they would do. And it makes both of them dearer to me than ever."

Again the tears welled and again she blinked them away.

"Your father certainly won't attempt anything before tomorrow," Larribee said, hiding his own feelings in gruffness again. "And I'll head him off as soon as he hits town. He's a sensible man, and will listen to me. Now about you. You came to town alone?"

"Yes."

"You're not going back that way."

"And why not?"

"Because I'm riding with you," Larribee told her.

Color was swiftly back in her face, her eyes dry and full of the old, independent, glinting spirit.

"I've ridden this range alone, day and night, for years and years. Nothing has ever happened to me, nothing ever will. And just why you persist in seeing me as some fragile, helpless sort of creature, I can't understand. Why do you?"

"Perhaps I don't," said Larribee quietly. "It could be that I'd like to see you home just for the pleasure it would give me to ride with you. Have you any objections to that?"

She turned to the door, flushing. She kept her back turned while she spoke, and her voice was low, subdued.

"To refuse would make me pretty ungrateful, wouldn't it? So you may ride with me. I'll be waiting at the river ford."

12

They rode in a silence that held for a full mile. Then it was Kelsey Fredericks who spoke, her words faintly amused, faintly jeering.

"He said he would see me home. Seeing is right. The man's a mute."

"Not that bad," Jim Larribee differed. "I just happened to be thinking. About how I once held down a line camp for a winter, all by myself. There wasn't much to do except put in time, so I borrowed a flock of books from a schoolmarm and did myself a heap of reading. I had to ride ten miles each way to get those books, but they sure were worth it. Looking back now, I figure it as one of the best winters of my life."

"How lucky for you there happened to be a schoolmarm," Kelsey said.

There was the faintest of edges in her words, which made Larribee glance at her. She sat her saddle with the light ease and certainty of one who had ridden all her life. She carried her head erect, slightly back and with her chin out, so that the thin silver glow of the stars touched her face fully, high-lighting it to an almost sculptured beauty.

"She was," Larribee drawled, "a mighty nice lady. Good looking, too. You'd never have guessed she was better than fifty years old."

Silence held again for another half mile, silence except for the steady mutter of jogging hoofs against the earth and the soft creak of saddle gear.

"So you spent a winter in a line camp and you read some books," Kelsey prompted. "Maybe you're still thinking about what you read?"

"Maybe. I often do. A lot of it was way over my head, but a little of it stuck. Funny how a thing like that can be. You read a whole book and out of it all there'll be just one line that stays with you."

"As for instance?"

" 'This the understanding silence and the heart's reward,' " quoted Larribee slowly.

It was Kelsey's turn to flash a quick and startled glance. Larribee, looking straight ahead, went on.:

"I forgot the name of the fellow who wrote that, but I sure liked the way he said things."

Wary of where such talk was leading, Kelsey did no more prompting, instead stirring her mount to a faster pace. The silence came down once more and held while they rode out the long miles of the valley, finally reaching and climbing the low slope of the stretch of "hungry land," as John Fredericks had called it. From the crest of this, the lights of the Fredericks ranch headquarters flickered way up ahead in the night. Kelsey reined to a stop.

"I'll go on alone from here," she said.

Off to one side in the dark a throat was gruffly cleared, and then Len Hobart's voice came to them, faintly apologetic.

"I ain't trying to eavesdrop, but you rode right up on me."

"Len!" Kelsey exclaimed. "What are you doing out here?"

"Worrying about you, for one thing. Then, what with this and that going on, I figure it don't hurt to keep an eye on things. So I was sort of prowling."

"Is Dad home yet?"

"Wasn't when I left a little bit ago. If you don't want him to know you been ridin', you better light a shuck."

For a moment, Kelsey did not answer. Then she turned to Larribee. "Thanks for everything, Jim."

With that she was gone, whipping away into the night, the mutter of her horse's hoofs a swift fading echo.

Len Hobart came up out of the gloom on foot, leading his horse. Larribee stepped from his saddle, got out his smoking and built a cigarette. He proffered tobacco and papers to Hobart.

"Your turn to smoke off me, Len."

"That girl—that Kelsey," Hobart said slowly. "She oughtn't ride alone so much, least of all at night, the way things are in the valley. After

Samuels going bad the way he did, there's no telling what'll be next."

"I've tried to tell her the same thing," Larribee agreed. "But there's a streak of independence in her a yard wide, and she's not afraid of anything concerning herself. She came to town tonight to see me about her father."

"What about him?"

"She's afraid he'll go after Big Dan Sharples and call him; that he'll go alone and be ganged by Dobe Lear and Curly Gibson. She asked me to head him off if he tried it."

"If John Fredericks really makes up his mind to go after Big Dan, there won't be anything stop him," Hobart said.

"There is still law in this valley," Larribee stated bluntly. "And I'm here to enforce it. That means I'll stop John Fredericks or anybody else from going on a gun rampage, so far as I can. You might talk sense to Fredericks if you see the signs building up."

"Yeah, I might"—agreed Hobart—"if I wanted to. But maybe I don't want to. Maybe I see it this way. I've been riding for John Fredericks a long time. I know how much he's put up with from Big Dan Sharples. It's Sharples who keeps this thing alive, who keeps the pressure on, who keeps hunting the trouble one way or another. I'm not saying this because I work for John Fredericks and because I like him plenty as a man. And I ain't saying it because I hate Big Dan's shadow. I'm saying it because it is the plain damn' truth!"

Len Hobart took a deep drag on his cigarette, the tip of it glowing bright.

"A man can stand being gnawed at just so long," he went on. "Then something in him busts loose and he sets out to settle things, once and for all. And you can't blame him."

"Maybe I can't blame him," Larribee said. "But I still got to stop him. I got no other choice. Besides, John Fredericks could very well come out of that sort of thing a dead man. And where's the sense in such a deal?"

Again the tip of Len Hobart's cigarette was a spark of ruby fire in the dark.

"When John Fredericks first hit this valley it was a chunk of frontier about as raw and wild as what you could find anywhere. And he didn't build up to what he is now by bein' a clumsy hand with a gun. He could surprise a lot of people, including Big Dan Sharples and all his handy men."

"That may be," Larribee admitted. "But did you ever think of it this way, Len? That the very thing Big Dan wants is to spur Fredericks into making such a break, and then have him ganged, just as Kelsey fears. That would leave Fredericks dead and Big Dan in the clear. He'd claim self-defense, have proof that Fredericks started the ball, and there matters would stand. If there is any one thing I've found out since I started wearing the star, it is that Big Dan Sharples is as smooth as they come—and as ruthless. He schemes all the time and he schemes deep, and always toward the future benefit of Big Dan Sharples."

Pinching out the butt of his cigarette, Larribee stepped into his saddle, then held up for a final remark.

"Len, you'll be smart if you do all you can to keep John Fredericks away from any try at a personal showdown with Big Dan. Good night!"

Hours after Jim Larribee had ridden away, Len Hobart was still out there on the crest of the "hungry land," hunkered on his heels, brooding over an endless succession of cigarettes. Long since had the last light faded from the windows of the home headquarters out yonder, which meant that John Fredericks had returned from Star Cross. Now the ranch lay asleep.

Hobart was thinking of the time he first met John Fredericks, years before, when he'd ridden in and asked for a job. Fredericks had looked him sternly in the eye for several long moments, then nodded and hired him. Fredericks hadn't sought to pry or ask a lot of questions. He had just made a judgment, hired a hand and let it go at that. Nor had he ever since tried to push into the private past of a man. Perhaps he understood how a man might want to forget the past, and live only in the goodness of the present and the future. . . .

In any event, Len Hobart had come to know a deep and unspoken fidelity to John Fredericks and all his affairs, such as he'd never known for any other man. The years he had spent riding for John Fredericks, Hobart reflected, had been the best years of his life. And the ranch had come nearer being a real home to him than any he'd ever known.

Then there was Kelsey! It was a strange thing, the deep affection he felt for Kelsey. Because it was a completely selfless thing, a prideful thing, as though she were his own daughter, and he could exult in her fineness and her beauty.

Keeping his self-imposed and solitary vigil out there under the midnight stars, Len Hobart thought of all these things, and he thought too of what Jim Larribee had said, just before riding back to town. About Big Dan Sharples, and how he could be scheming to force John Fredericks past the edge and then have him ganged by such as Dobe Lear and Curly Gibson. And it was with these thoughts that Len Hobart came to his decision.

There was but one sure way to clear up this whole thing. That was for him, Len Hobart, to ride to town, walk in on Big Dan Sharples, throw a gun and finish it, then and there. No matter what came to him after that, it would be worth the price. He would have paid John Fredericks fully for the good years of living he had known. And he would have removed the cloud of fear from Kelsey's mind.

Yeah, it was a good idea, the best kind of idea! And when a better time than the present?

Len Hobart stood up, stretched, filled his lungs with night's good, keen breath. He had his look at the stars and made his guess at the hour. Well past midnight, he decided. But plenty of time to amble in toward town and move in on Big Dan Sharples real early in the morning, when he'd be least expecting trouble. . . .

He turned to his horse and swung up. The horse, long since impatient for the home corral, started to lift into a jog in that direction, but Hobart hauled the animal around and sent it downvalley and at a long westward slant toward the river, settling himself solidly back against the cantle for the ride to town. Yet within a short quarter mile he was reining sharply up, while standing in his stirrups and leaning forward, head slightly turned as he listened.

To his straining ears it came again, a thin clamor of complaint. Sheep, by God! Beyond any doubt—sheep!

Hobart dug in his spurs, racing to meet the sound. Abruptly there was the high, black bulk of a big freight wagon towering above him, and in his nostrils a hot animal smell that was unmistakable. Sheep!

He set his horse back to a skidding halt, and sent a harsh, challenging yell rocketing.

"This is Len Hobart. You up there—who are you? Where you think you're going with these damned woollies? This is cattle range, and no sheep stop here. You hear me? Speak up, name yourself!"

The lumbering roll of the wagon came to a halt, and farther back, more brake blocks squealed as a second wagon stopped. Then it was Joe Lollard's voice that came down to Hobart from the box of the lead wagon, and it was a voice full of anxious apology.

"This is Joe Lollard, and I don't own no sheep. I'm just a mule skinner, workin' for Ira Redstone and takin' his orders. And from now on—let go my arm, Forbush! Let go, I tell you! I ain't takin' a curryin' for you or nobody else! My hide's mine, and I ain't riskin' a hole in it for no load of damn' stinkin' sheep. So hold it, Hobart. I'm comin' off this wagon, and comin' peaceful. Hold it—!"

Came the thump of boot heels hitting the earth. Joe Lollard had come all the way off the wagon box in one jump. After landing he fell forward on hands and knees and stayed that way for a little time, jarred, shaken and breathless.

But still up there on the wagon box, Ed Forbush was a humped shape against the stars, and he was sending down his voiced defiance.

"I got a right to haul these sheep wherever I—"

"With sheep, at this end of the valley you ain't got a right in the world, Forbush," cut in Len Hobart. "Come down off that wagon. And I won't tell you twice!"

Forbush's reply was a nasal drone. "Hobart, you just ain't that big!"

Len Hobart and his horse made a shadowy blot, down there against earth's blackness, but Forbush figured he had him located close enough, so now the gun Forbush had been snaking stealthily into the clear, spat its flame and its hard, round report, and a smashing force caught at Len Hobart, wrenching him savagely, knocking him out of his saddle. His horse spun away to one side, snorting its gusty alarm.

The impact of his fall to earth did several things to Len Hobart. First, it savagely hurt a bullet-shattered left shoulder, but it was this pain that burned through the mists of daze and shock and left his faculties starkly sharp and clear. And so he saw up above him, against the stars, the outleaning figure of Ed Forbush, and he drew his gun and lifted it into line.

Forbush was yelling at Joe Lollard, damning him for a coward, ordering him back up on the wagon, and adding that maybe now a lot of wise bastards, including that star-packing Jim Larribee, would get over the idea they could go on pushing Ed Forbush around forever. And he'd take sheep anywhere he goddam pleased, and if anybody tried to stop him they'd get the same dose he'd just given—!

From where Len Hobart lay, deep in earth's dark shadows, a finger of gun flame, fast winking, lanced upward, and gun report was a rolling gust of sound. But Ed Forbush neither saw the flame or heard the report, for, speeding ahead of both was the bullet that smashed the bridge of his nose and chewed its shattering way through his narrow skull. He came down off the wagon box in a limp, pouring fall, striking on his head and shoulders, his gangling legs whipping over in a crooked, sprawling arc. He never moved again.

Mules, weary though they were from the long haul, spun nervously around to the left, cramping the wagon wheels hard over, jumping and trampling the swinging, clanking chain.

Back on the second wagon, young Henry Jeffers heard Len Hobart's first challenge. He heard Joe Lollard's answer, and he heard the words between Hobart and Ed Forbush. And after that the guns. And so now the decision he'd been considering ever since leaving Trent's Meadow became a concrete thing.

All along the night haul, Henry had been thinking on this, and revulsion over his part in the affair had grown and grown. Sheep on Concho Creek! Certain trouble. Another blow aimed at people he liked and admired, like John Fredericks and old Tasker Gentry, and particularly at Sheriff Jim Larribee, who would be caught between the two forces and could well be crucified there.

Also, Henry's revulsion had grown toward the man riding beside him, this fellow Shack Kincheloe: for Kincheloe had bragged and blown all along the way, a dozen times reminding Henry that he, Shack Kincheloe, had a stake in this sheep deal, that he'd give orders and take no back talk from anybody, particularly from any damn wet-eared young mule skinner. And if anybody wanted to argue the point with a gun, then he, Shack Kincheloe, would be right there to oblige.

Henry Jeffers was the sort to anger slowly, but mightily. He was angry now. So, when first harsh words and then harsh guns echoed up ahead in the night, and Shack Kincheloe leaned forward and across in front of Henry in an effort to see what was going on, Henry drove the point of a shrewdly swung elbow into Kincheloe's throat, setting him back, gagging and choking. While he was in this shape, Henry slammed him full on his bony jaw with a lashing right fist.

Shack Kincheloe toppled off the wagon box, and even as he struck the ground, Henry Jeffers was down there on top of him, locating Kincheloe's jaw by feel, then belting it savagely a full half-dozen times before realizing his man was unresisting and fully out. After which he took Kincheloe's gun and threw it far out into the darkness.

He moved along beside his string of mules, quieting them, then cut between the leaders and the back of Joe Lollard's wagon, calling Joe's name. Joe's answer came, shaken and subdued.

"All right, Henry—all right!"

"That shooting," Henry said. "Anybody hurt?"

"Yeah," came Len Hobart's voice, tight and quiet. "I got a hole in my shoulder, and Forbush is down there by the wagon. I've a feeling he's done for. You're Jeffers?"

"That's right. Like Joe Lollard, I had no idea what we were getting into when we started. Then we had no choice."

Henry scratched a match, took a quick look at the lank, sprawled figure by the off front wheel of the wagon. He caught his breath, pinched out the match, crossed over to Len Hobart.

"You're right about Forbush," he said, his voice a trifle unsteady. "Now what about you?"

"Bring my bronc over here and give me a leg up," Hobart said. "Then I'll get back to headquarters. It ain't too far."

"Maybe you can't last it."

"I'll last it. It's not that bad with me. Get my bronc."

Len Hobart's horse had swung in by the mules, stayed close to them, and Henry had no trouble catching a trailing rein. With Joe Lollard helping, he got Len Hobart to his feet, then to his saddle, feeling the warm stickiness of Hobart's blood on his hands.

"You sure you can make it alone?" he asked anxiously.

"Yeah," Hobart gritted. "I'll make it. I'll sure as hell make it! What do you figger to do with the woollies? You can't unload them around here."

"We won't," promised Henry. "Joe and me, we'll haul them back to town and let Redstone worry about the rest."

"Fair enough," murmured Hobart. "Fair enough."

He touched his horse with the spur and moved off into the night. Henry stared after him, scrubbing his hands up and down on the legs of his jeans to get that clammy stickiness off them. And silently he marveled at the tenacity that could lie in the human spirit. . . .

Joe Lollard tugged at Henry's elbow.

"What we goin' to do, Henry? Me, I feel like leavin' everything just like she is, and gettin' the hell out. This arguin' and shootin' and killin' just ain't for me. I ain't mad at nobody or anything. Yes, sir—I feel like leavin' everything just as she is."

"But we're not going to, Joe," Henry said. "We're going to tie up a live man and load him on one wagon. We're going to load a dead man on the other and take everything back to the home corrals in town. The rest of it will be up to Ira Redstone. All right—lend a hand. We got things to do and miles to travel!"

13

Dawn broke grayly over the town of Silver Ford. With its arrival came also the rumble of heavy freighter wheels and the thin, persistent crying of thirst-punished sheep. By habit an early riser, Big Dan Sharples had stirred up a fire in his kitchen stove and cooked the first pot of coffee for the day. He was sipping at a cup of this as he made his way into the store and through the chill gloom of the place to unlock and swing wide the front door. Immediately to his ears came the complaint of the sheep.

He went quickly to the edge of the store porch and stared down Valley Street. There, at Ira Redstone's stage and freight corrals, the two big freighters that had rolled out of Silver Ford late yesterday, were just hauling to a halt. This would have been all right, had they been empty. But they weren't. It was from them that the sound of the sheep came, sheep that should, by this time, have been grazing along Concho Creek.

What had gone wrong? What in hell could have gone wrong?

Big Dan whirled back into the store, hurried to an iron-faced door that led into his warehouse, where, in a walled-off corner, Dobe Lear and Curly Gibson had their bunks and did their sleeping. Both were just beginning to stir, and Big Dan's harsh summons brought them fully up in their blankets.

"Dobe! Get down to Redstone's layout and see what the hell went wrong? Why the sheep are still in the wagons instead of out on Concho Creek? Hurry up!"

Dobe pulled on his shirt and jeans, reached for his boots. Big Dan went back to the kitchen, poured himself more coffee, gulped it almost scalding hot. A vast anger and an equally vast sense of frustration peaked up inside him. Here, plainly, was another plan that had somehow gone awry. Just why it had, he did not know, but definitely awry it was. So many things, he thought savagely, had suddenly begun going wrong, starting with the defiance and defection of Sheriff Jim Larribee.

Previous to that, virtually every move he had plotted and put into effect down across the years toward the great objective—the destruction of John Fredericks and all his works—had gone smoothly and surely. To a point. To the point where Jim Larribee slipped away from his grip and influence.

Like just yesterday, when the word had come of Boardy Samuels' sudden finish, and why. And ever since there had been the lurking fear that Boardy might have been whipsawed into some kind of disclosures before he had made his blindly desperate try, and so died in front of Jim Larribee's gun. And if Boardy had talked, had he mentioned the name of Big Dan Sharples—?

This was a thought which had harried Big Dan for a greater part of the night just past, and though he had tried to put it out of mind, it had clung like a pallid ghost.

To balance somewhat the effect of this, had been the thought that morning would see sheep on Concho Creek. A relatively small flock, sure enough, but the beginning of a woolly tide that would flow and flow until it rolled John Fredericks under. Sheep! Brute stubborn and persistent; hard to contain and get rid of, once they gained a start. Not so easily made fearful and moved out as were men whose allegiance had to be bought, and which reached no farther than the cold dollars and cents involved.

Yeah—sheep! And in given time, a thousand of them—two thousand—five thousand! Feeding along Concho Creek and all across the range that had belonged to John Fredericks. Complete conquest, complete fulfillment of the great hate, and a full measure of financial profit besides. That was what was to come, once the start was made.

But the start hadn't been made. The sheep that were to have been the start were not on Concho Creek. Instead, they were still in those two freight wagons, downstreet. . . .

Big Dan poured more coffee, and reached for the whisky bottle to add a strong measure of that to the cup. For deep inside him premonition had taken shape and begun to stir; a gray and chilling thing which whispered the possibility of failure.

Failure! The thought of it had never before entered his mind. It did not seem possible that he could fail, for he had always planned and calculated so carefully, and down across the years he had seen all his desired moves work out successfully. He had seen John Fredericks pushed ever steadily farther and farther back in the valley, had seen him and Tasker Gentry contained more completely with every passing year. Tasker Gentry, of course, did not now and never would count heavily in this thing. He was incidental, but the tie of his friendship for Fredericks would eventually doom him too. No, there had been no failure over the past years. But now—!

The door opened and Dobe Lear came in, out of breath from hurrying. Big Dan whirled on him.

"Well?"

"Sheep there, all right," Dobe panted. "Two full wagons of them. And Ed Forbush, he's dead. While Shack—"

"What!" Big Dan ripped out the word. "Forbush dead? You sure?"

"Plumb! I saw Larribee and young Jeffers and Joe Lollard liftin' him down off one of the wagons. He was plenty dead. And accordin' to what Jeffers was tellin' Larribee, it was that Fredericks rider, Len Hobart, who killed him, and that after Forbush had winged Hobart some. Shack Kincheloe, he's some beat up and plenty hangdog, with the look of havin' lost all his salt and nerve. You want I should go back for another look and listen, boss?"

"No, not now, Dobe," Big Dan said heavily. Inside him, that gray and haunting premonition was constantly growing. "You and Curly stick around. Close!"

Downstreet, at Ira Redstone's corrals, they had carried the body of Ed Forbush into the stage station, herding Shack Kincheloe ahead of them. They laid Ed Forbush down against a wall and covered him with a blanket which a hurriedly dressed and still sleep-heavy Redstone produced.

Jim Larribee, himself disheveled, had been awakened by the jolting rumble of the big wagons and the penetrating discordancy of the sheep complaint. He had jumped into his clothes and hurried to investigate and listened to Henry Jeffers' terse account of the previous night's happenings. Now, bleak of eye, he put his words on Ira Redstone.

"All right, let's have what *you* know, Redstone. Who owns the sheep in those wagons? And who hired the wagons for the haul to Concho Creek?"

Redstone was a little slow with his answer, considering it carefully. There was no depth of virtue in Ira Redstone; where his immediate interests were concerned, he would not shy away from venality. Also, there was a certain dull stolidity in him that could nurture and maintain a lengthy hate. For a long time he had secretly despised Big Dan Sharples. While for business reasons he had bent the knee to Big Dan, he had always resented the need of having to endure Big Dan's domineering arrogance and sarcasm. And he had always hoped for the chance to aid in humbling Big Dan and cutting him down to size. Perhaps now was the time.

For, over the past few days, he had seen a crack appear in Big Dan's armor, and glimpsed uncertainty beyond. This had happened on that morning when, on the porch of the Acme Mercantile, Jim Larribee had defied Big Dan to his teeth, when he had whipsawed Big Dan into a lie and held him cornered there.

That day Big Dan had blustered and threatened, but in the end backed down fully before Larribee's cold anger and contempt. So perhaps now was a good time to start getting over to the other side of the creek. . . . Redstone cleared night's thickness from his throat.

"Big Dan hired the wagons. I'm not sure who owns the sheep. Sharples must have some interest in them."

"Did you know the wagons were going out to haul sheep?" Larribee demanded.

Redstone's eyes shifted. He shrugged. "I knew. But what the hell! It's my business to hire out wagons and mules and skinners. Should Fredericks or Gentry want to hire an outfit of mine, all they got to do is speak the word. I play no favorites."

"A statement I could question," Larribee said coldly. He turned to Shack Kincheloe.

"Maybe you know. Does Big Dan Sharples own those sheep?"

"Some," Kincheloe mumbled.

"The rest?"

"I do."

"Partnership deal, eh? You're new around here. Didn't Sharples tell you that any attempt to put sheep in the north end of the valley would stir up serious trouble?"

"I didn't deal with Sharples direct," Kincheloe said. "It was all arranged through Forbush. And he said that while there might be a little argument with a couple of cow outfits, Sharples would see to it that the law would back our hand. He said Sharples was lining up a new sheriff who would work with us."

"So-o!" murmured Larribee sardonically. "Did Forbush, by any chance, mention the name of this new sheriff?"

"Yeah. Said it was a feller by the name of Samuels, Boardy Samuels. Forbush said this Samuels had been sheriff once before, but that he'd tried to ride the wrong horse, so lost out. Said he knew better now that he'd found out where the real weight lay in the valley, and that he'd work along with us and keep the cow outfits off our necks."

"Nice arrangement, had it worked," Larribee said harshly. "But it happens that Samuels is dead." He put his glance on Ira Redstone again. "You knew about all this?"

Redstone shrugged again, did not answer.

To Henry Jeffers, Larribee said, "You've had a long night of it, boy—you and Joe. Are you up to taking those sheep back to where you picked them up?"

Henry nodded. "And you understand that Joe and me, we had no idea what we were getting into? If we had, we'd never have started out in the first place."

Larribee dropped a hand on Henry's arm. "Sure—I know. Take this fellow with you and dump him off with the sheep." He indicated Shack Kincheloe, then spoke to Kincheloe directly. "I advise you to get out of this valley with your sheep. And once gone—stay so!"

He turned to leave. Redstone jerked his head toward the blanket-covered figure of Ed Forbush.

"What about him?"

"I'll leave it to you to locate Doc Shields," Larribee said curtly. "Doc will know what to do."

Angling up and across the street, Jim Larribee

moved a little heavily, a little wearily. For the knowledge he now possessed and the logical conclusions to be drawn from it were a somber weight upon him. Now he knew the reason for Boardy Samuels' furtive contact with Big Dan Sharples. Now he knew why Fitch Gentry had died, treacherously shot in the back by Boardy. It was a price Big Dan had demanded, and one Boardy had been willing to pay, so that he might again wear the star.

Why should Big Dan have wanted Fitch killed? There was but one logical answer. Why else than to point a black finger at Sheriff Jim Larribee? To make it appear that, having located Fitch and hating him for the getaway he'd made at Sweetwater Glade, Larribee had deliberately gunned him, instead of bringing him back to town in lawful custody. And so had forfeited all chance of support from Tasker Gentry and John Fredericks.

Yes, that would be it, a perfect example of the kind of coldly ruthless, iniquitous scheming at which Big Dan Sharples had shown he was so adept. But it was a scheme that hadn't worked, because young Henry Jeffers had heard the shots that killed Fitch Gentry and investigated, thus proving the time Fitch had died. And at the exact time, Jim Larribee was in town, long miles from the place.

Larribee paused at his office door. Day had

come on quickly, once it had begun to fully brighten. Over beyond the Sabines the strong fires of sunrise were massing. Down at the freight corrals, Henry Jeffers and Joe Lollard had climbed again to their lofty seats on the boxes of the towering freighters. The man Kincheloe was a humped and subdued figure beside Henry Jeffers. The mules leaned into the pull, the chains lifted and tightened and the wagons stirred and lumbered away, carrying the odor and sound of their contents into morning's far distance.

Larribee went on into his office, to the back room where he slept. While he shaved and washed up, the first measure of conviction of what he must do took form in his mind and began to grow. And the more he considered and weighed this conviction from all angles the more grim became his decision.

Fully apparent was the fact that Big Dan Sharples would never, of his own accord, call a halt to his perverted, dedicated purpose of eventually destroying John Fredericks. Also, despite the disclosures wrung from Shack Kincheloe, there was no way to strike legally at Big Dan. There was no solid evidence that could be produced to prove him directly tied in with the killing of Fitch Gentry. For Boardy Samuels was dead and Ed Forbush likewise, and so there was no direct witness to anything.

Yes, out of last night's happenings, Ed Forbush

lay dead, and up at the Fredericks ranch was Len Hobart with a bullet-smashed shoulder. Henry Jeffers had said he thought Hobart not too seriously hurt, but that was merely a guess with no certainty in it. Perhaps by this time Len Hobart was gone too.

Dead men—hurt men! Fitch Gentry. Boardy Samuels. Ed Forbush. Len Hobart surely wounded. Grant Hilliker still in bed, recovering from a brutally savage beating . . .

And behind all this the malignant touch of Big Dan Sharples. Where next would the curse of this man's hate strike?

Finished with his shave and wash, Jim Larribee combed his hair carefully. The face looking back at him from the small wall mirror was edged with a graven soberness. It was a face that had grown considerably older during the past two weeks.

He donned his hat, buckled on his gun and went out into the sunrise, which poured its slanting glitter straight up River Street. Larribee, tipping his head against the strong flare as he reached the White Stag corner and turned in there, did not see John Fredericks ride in across the ford and stop in front of Abe Chain's livery barn.

In the White Stag, Morrie Carr poured a cup of coffee and shoved it across the counter, then stood awaiting Larribee's order. He got it and went back to his stove. Larribee sugared his coffee and began sipping it, glad that Morrie hadn't tried to stir up some line of idle talk.

Bacon sputtered in the pan, giving off its own rich fragrance. Shortly it was joined by the thin crackle of frying eggs, and then Morrie was putting Larribee's breakfast before him. At that moment the door of the place swung and it was little Abe Chain who came hurrying in.

"Jim!" he called. "Jim!"

Larribee swung around. "What is it, Abe?"

"Maybe nothin', maybe a lot. John Fredericks, he just rode up to my place, left his horse with me. There was a look about him I never saw before. Kind of cold and far away. And stern, like maybe God would be stern. And here's what he said: 'Keep an eye on my horse, Abe. I'll either be back for it shortly—or I never will.' That's what he said, Jim, and the way he looked and the way he said that made me feel like mebbe the whole world was due to cave in. I—I figgered I better tell you."

Larribee was already halfway to the door.

"Where did he go from your place, Abe?"

"The Acme Mercantile."

Jim Larribee crossed River Street at a run, cut past the corner of the Acme Mercantile porch, then went up the steps in two long leaps. The slanting sun rays laid a path of light well beyond the open door of the place, and Larribee plunged through this, his senses taut and reaching.

In the shadowed depths of the big store, John Fredericks was speaking, and his words carried a flat finality.

"I told you how it would be, Dan. I warned you that if you struck at me again, and brought injury to me or mine, then would I come after you—direct! Right now my best and most faithful rider, Len Hobart, is lying in his bunk out at the ranch, a bullet through his shoulder. He's not going to die, but he'll probably carry a stiff shoulder the rest of his life. You're responsible for that, just as much as if you'd fired the shot yourself. Dan, you've lived too long, injured too many good men. Now it ends. I offer you an even break, no more. Go for it!"

Free of the glare of the door, Jim Larribee saw now how it was. Big Dan Sharples stood behind the long counter. He had been sorting out the day's change and putting it in the cash drawer, which stood open in front of him. Across the counter, John Fredericks faced him. Farther along, old Charley Clark stood, silent and watchful and thoroughly neutral.

Larribee's glance sought Dobe Lear and Curly Gibson, and found only Dobe, who was a small, waspy, venomous shape, half crouched in the doorway that led back to Big Dan's living quarters. Dobe was plainly cocked and primed, his glance fixed unwinkingly on John Fredericks, his teeth showing between tight-pulled lips in a soundless snarl.

In Big Dan's hooded eyes as he faced John Fredericks was all the accumulated hate of the years, hate that was a raw and blazing light. This wasn't the way Big Dan wanted it, but this, he realized now, was the way it would have to be. He knew John Fredericks well enough to understand this was no bluff on the cattleman's part. Here was the finish, one way or another. Here, after all the years of planning and maneuvering was what it all boiled down to. How much simpler it all would have been, had it come to this years ago! A gray fatalism came over him.

There was a big-bored, snub-barreled gun in the cash drawer. It had always been there and always loaded. Could he get it in time? He had to try. And if he could maneuver just a little edge—!

"Get him, Dobe!" he growled.

As he spoke, Big Dan grabbed for the cash-drawer gun.

Knowing the moment he entered the store that he had no chance of heading off this thing, that he had a choice to make, and that there was only one choice he could make, Jim Larribee was set and ready for what he knew must surely come. Now, with Big Dan's words, he went for his gun, his attention strictly on Dobe Lear.

He saw Dobe Lear make his draw, and knew

Dobe meant to get John Fredericks from the side. So he sent his shot at Dobe and put a bullet angling through the waspy little gunman, heart-high. Dobe, knocked sideways, seemed to hang against the doorpost, where he got off his shot, which plowed a splintery furrow along the counter top between John Fredericks and Big Dan Sharples. Within the next breath, Dobe Lear was just a huddled little pile in the doorway.

As close as an echo behind Dobe's try came a third shot, heavy and final, and it blared from the muzzle of the big black gun that had appeared in the hand of John Fredericks.

Big Dan had got the cash-drawer gun—had it clear, but now seemed struck with some sort of paralysis. Twice he opened his mouth as if to speak, twice he closed it without making a sound. A little shift of movement went through him. His fingers loosened and the gun he held dropped back into the cash drawer, unfired.

Big Dan pressed his hand to his body and began to bend slowly forward until it seemed his face would strike the counter top. Abruptly his legs went out from under him and his ponderous torso slid sideways along the edge of the counter and dropped from sight beyond in a heavy, muffled impact.

Jim Larribee half stepped, half jumped past Dobe Lear's crumpled figure, and went on swiftly into Big Dan's living quarters, still mindful that

Curly Gibson must be about somewhere. Curly was. He was in the kitchen, again soaking his bad hand in a bucket of hot water. This time, when Larribee appeared, he made no hostile move nor uttered a hostile word. He merely lifted both hands on the level with his ears. Larribee could see that the right one was still badly swollen.

Curly still carried strong signs of the going over he'd taken at Larribee's hands. There was a pallor beneath the weather tan and bruises on his face, while far back in his eyes lay the shadow of a strong fear, now also showing in his voice.

"Whatever went, out front, I'm not in it—not in it at all!"

Larribee's nod was curt.

"Fair enough. But you're leaving the Pride River Valley, Curly. For good. You got until sundown. Don't be anywhere around here after that!"

"I won't," Curly said.

He dried his hand on a soiled towel, took his hat off the table and moved to the back door. Here he paused.

"Dobe?"

"Done for."

"Big Dan?"

"The same."

Curly considered a moment, then shrugged. "It was bound to come. The signs were up."

"What signs?" Larribee asked.

"Just—the signs." Then Curly Gibson was gone, closing the door carefully behind him.

"I doubt I could have headed it off, even had I wanted to, Grant," Jim Larribee said. "The point is, I didn't want to. As sheriff I should have been strictly neutral and made at least some sort of try at halting the affair. Instead, I sided John Fredericks and was glad of the chance. I know now that I never would be able to see the law in the strict balance and perfection you do; I know that I would always take sides, going along with men I liked against those I didn't, regardless of the merits of the case."

Sitting up in bed, Grant Hilliker drew carefully on the first cigar Hannah Virgil had allowed him since his misadventure at the hands of Curly Gibson.

"That is an entirely human and commendable trait," he said slowly. "Standing up for your friends, I mean. However, given time, you'd learn to keep it in balance where your official duties are concerned."

Larribee shook his head.

"No, I never would. And that's only one of the reasons why I'm taking off the star."

"You have others, then?"

"Several. Do you know what I halfway had in mind, Grant, even before John Fredericks hit town? Well, it was to do exactly what he did, without anywhere near his justification. I was considering whipsawing Big Dan Sharples into a break, then killing him. I was going to be judge, jury and executioner. I was going to step completely outside my oath of office. And any man capable of that kind of thinking has no business wearing a star."

Through the smoke of his cigar, Grant Hilliker peered up at Larribee with a narrowed, quizzical glance.

"You're talking off the top of your head. You'd never have gone through with anything as extreme as that."

"I'm not so sure," retorted Larribee soberly. "At any rate, I've taken a pretty thorough look at myself, and I know I'd never be fully happy in office. For the star builds a wall around a man, puts a limit to his personal freedom. Whether or not he wants it so, it herds him off in a corner by himself, a corner that can be damned lonely, as I've found out. Finally, there's a way of life I like better."

"Such as?"

"What I set out to be when I first came into this valley. Maybe a shoestring cattleman to begin with, but always with the chance of someday being a forty-dollar-pair-of-boots cattleman. I got a cabin waiting for me on Concho Creek, and when I'm in it I'll be completely my own man again."

"If you surrender the star, Jim, you'll make Ira Redstone and Bert Carter happy."

"To the contrary. Both of them have already been to see me, urging me to stay on. With the weight of Big Dan off their necks, they're very humble and anxious to please everybody."

"They're climbing on the band wagon, you mean," Hilliker remarked cynically. "Ah, well—it takes all kinds." He drew in a big mouthful of smoke, savored it luxuriously, then let it out with a long, sighing breath. A faint smile pulled at his lips. "My good and valued friend, you are a very fundamental man, and seem to know your own measure exactly. So who am I to try and change your mind?"

Larribee left Hannah Virgil's yard through the blue shadows of another early forming dusk. The town was quiet. All day it had seethed with excitement, for word of the momentous decision worked out in gunsmoke in the Acme Mercantile had spread far and fast, and men from all over the valley and back in the hills had ridden in to get the certainty of it, to learn all the details. Now they had gone their several ways again, and Silver Ford lay quiet in the dusk, sober and hushed.

It was, mused Jim Larribee, like a storm that had gathered, burst in wild fury, then gone away; a breeze that had peaked to a hurricane, blasting the lives and destinies of men into new ways and patterns, leaving some dead and some alive, and with certain problems solved for all time.

Crossing River Street and pausing at the White Stag corner, Larribee saw the lank figure of Henry Jeffers come up from the freight yard and stop at the door of the Rojas home. The door opened to Henry's knock, and there appeared the quick-gleaming smile and shining eyes of Rita Rojas in welcome. There was the sound of Henry's quiet, steady voice and Rita's swift, bright laughter. Then the door closed, and the town was still and empty once more.

In the office, Larribee lighted a lamp and began sorting the few odds and ends of stuff he'd accumulated. He went through the desk. There was no great deal of anything, save an official letter or two, a few circulars, some reward dodgers, none of which meant anything to him any more.

He fingered the star, unpinned it and laid it on the desk. Its small weight had become a familiar presence on his shirt front, and he'd once thought that if it were ever removed, it would leave him with a great sense of loss. It wasn't that way at all. Now he knew only relief, the sense of once more being fully free.

He looked around the room. What else? His saddle and other riding gear, his scabbarded rifle, all were down at Abe Chain's livery stable. His warbag was still at Hannah Virgil's place. He would, he decided, spend this one last night in town, then gather his gear in the morning and head out.

He spun up a cigarette and settled back in his chair. But swiftly he came to his feet again: for it was Kelsey Fredericks who stepped through the door.

"Who comes more often than I?" she said.

The residue of harshness which had been in Larribee's face all day, now softened out completely.

"And who more welcome?" he said gently.

She came farther into the room. "I rode by the cabin on Concho Creek. I thought I might find you there."

"Why did you think so?" Larribee asked.

She gave a small shrug, pointing to the star on the desk. "I knew that one day you'd decide to take that off. And I knew that when you did, the place you'd probably head for."

She was in her usual riding gear; divided skirt, snug buckskin jacket, a silk muffler about her throat. And tonight there was something more about her, an extra gleam of vitality and spirit.

"You are," Larribee said, "remarkably shrewd. And tonight, more lovely than ever."

She caught her breath, colored, then spoke swiftly.

"I came to thank you, Jim. I'm wondering if you gave up more than you should have when you stood beside Dad this morning? He told me all of it. Was the favor I asked of you last night beyond justness?"

"No," he told her slowly. "I'd have sided your father under any condition. It seems we never fully know ourselves until the big decision looks us right in the eye. Today has been one of decisions. And there is one more to be made, Kelsey Fredericks. It is for you to make it. Do I ride to Concho Creek or do I drift out of the Pride River Valley—for good?"

She knew what he meant. She knew exactly what he meant. Her head went back in the old characteristic manner, her glance holding his steadily for a long, throbbing moment. Then her eyes turned luminous and her mouth curved in sweetness. Direct as the flight of a homing bird she moved past the desk and close to him.

"It doesn't matter, Jim," she said softly. "Wherever you go, I'm going with you!"

Center Point Large Print
600 Brooks Road / PO Box 1
Thorndike, ME 04986-0001 USA

(207) 568-3717

US & Canada:
1 800 929-9108
www.centerpointlargeprint.com